EMERALDS AND ESPIONAGE

A Novel

Lynn Gardner

Covenant Communications, Inc.

Published by Covenant Communications, Inc.
American Fork, Utah

Printed in the United States of America
Third Printing: July 1998
98 99 00 01 02 10 9 8 7 6 5 4 3

ISBN 1-55530-771-2

Chapter One

The silver strand of beach, lit only by a thin crescent moon, stretched before me in the darkness. How long, how far I'd run, I didn't know. I'd lost track of time and miles as I tried to out distance the ghosts pursuing me. A good run cleared my head, put my problems in perspective, and enabled me to think and plan more clearly. Out of breath, heart pounding, I turned toward the estate.

My eyes focused on a dark shape in the white foamy surf. A small boat was beaching nearby.

As I approached, a man shouted. Ready for the usual questions— "Where are we?" and "Is this a private beach?"—I started toward the boat with the usual answers. Suddenly something whistled past my ear! I froze. A second shot ricocheted off the rock next to me.

I dove for cover. Someone was shouting, scrambling, stumbling over the rocks toward me. I crept behind a tall, jagged rock, then inched towards another, and another, distancing myself from the intruders, and when I had an open beach in front of me, ran—hard—not looking back.

I darted up the steep path that led from beach to hilltop, and racing across the lawn, plunged through the door of the darkened cottage. Locking it behind me, I slumped against the door, trembling in shock. When my legs stopped quivering, I checked the window to see if I'd been followed. Strangers would need a light to get up the trail from the beach. I saw none.

Was I safe here? Who were they? What were they doing on my beach? Why were they shooting at me?

I checked locks on doors and windows, then dashed upstairs to my bedroom balcony to listen for sounds of pursuit. All I heard was my own heartbeat.

Calm down, Allison. No one's coming.

Since I was alone on the estate, I left the cottage dark. If they didn't know about the house, I certainly wouldn't advertise it.

I crept down the dark stairs to the telephone. There was no dial tone. It was dead.

No! I forgot to call the phone company from the big house to have our phone turned on when I got back. The only phones working on the estate were across more than a thousand feet of lawn, and I wasn't about to leave the safety of my hidden cottage.

Mom would be frantic in Athens. She always called to make sure my flight from New York arrived safely in Los Angeles, and I'd found no problems on the estate.

Should I chance a run across the lawn? I felt my way back upstairs and listened on the balcony. *My imagination, or voices wafting on the wind?* Whatever it was, it determined my decision. I'd stay put, secure behind locked doors, hope the intruders actually were gone, and that Mom wouldn't send Milton chasing from New York to be with me.

I treasured this time alone on Margo's estate every year—at least, I had before. Maybe they were right, maybe it wasn't safe anymore.

Willing my tense, tired body to relax, and comforted slightly by the gun under my pillow, I lay awake a long time, listening, remembering . . .

Though it had been twenty years, the memory of hot tears burning streaks down my five-year-old cheeks was fresh. The War Department telegram had changed our lives drastically. An explosion in Vietnam, no body, my father was dead. I didn't believe it then. Nor now. There were too many impressions, an eerie sense of closeness to my father that belied the telegram. That's what brought me back to the estate year after year—to discover some clue that would prove he was alive.

When Jim and Alma, caretakers on Margo's estate, took their vacation each spring, I came home to Southern California to watch over things and continue my private search into the mystery of Margo's house, her life, and most of all, why I felt a connection to my father here. To my knowledge, my father had never been here.

Margo, absentee owner of my "home"—beautiful, talented star of delightful musicals of the '60s—had simply disappeared one Christmas after performing for the troops in Vietnam. Jim and Alma were instructed to keep her magnificent mansion ready for her return, and for years had faithfully done so.

After the telegram demolished our lives, Mom answered an ad to manage the estate, though her primary job remained at the college. I pictured Mom at the lectern, dark eyes sparkling with enthusiasm, her mane of lustrous dark hair forever escaping in wispy tendrils from the neat bun she struggled with every morning. Margaret Alexander was a recognized authority on native folklore and music, as well as a lecturer, author, and teacher.

Our cottage, nestled in giant Spanish oaks below Margo's

mansion, was cozy and snug. I ran free on hundreds of acres of rolling golden hills dotted with huge oak trees, and a private beach—miles of white sand punctuated by jagged rocks—where I came when I needed to sort out my life.

Who else came to this beach—my beach—to these rocks—and why had they shot at me? I finally drifted into a troubled sleep, waking at every sound.

I welcomed the radiance of the morning sun, its warmth and safety. *Safety from what?* I'd probably startled the intruders as much as they startled me. Except I didn't shoot at them!

I threw open the windows, flooding the house with golden sunshine and fresh air. It had been closed while Mom lectured in Greece and I was in New York, where my job as an interpreter at the United Nations kept me most of the time.

I'd better use my time wisely this morning. I didn't expect interruptions, but they always came, preventing me from finding the information I felt sure was hidden somewhere in that vast house. Grabbing an apple and a sweater, I got the keys to the big house from the roll-top desk by the door and hurried outside.

The morning was crisp and clear, dispelling my fright of the night before—until I saw a strange black ship beyond the cove. The hair prickled on the back of my neck and sent shivers through me. *Did those men come from this foreign-looking ship?*

Slipping back into the house, I grabbed the binoculars and made out Oriental characters on the bow—"Emerald of the East." It could have been an abandoned derelict for all the movement on board. There was probably no connection between the men last night and this unusual ship, but I had an eerie foreboding of danger. I felt someone was watching me, instead of me watching them.

Replacing the binoculars, I locked the door behind me.

I can't believe this. You never lock the doors when you are on the estate! But, after all, I had promised I would be careful and alert. *Why had that word sounded so strange coming from Milton?* Probably because my staid, very proper fiance didn't usually think in those terms. Careful, yes. Alert? It had given me goose bumps when he said it.

I jogged the few hundred yards to the big house, the sun warming my head, the grass wet with heavy dew. Slipping out of my soggy shoes, I left them by the door.

The grand foyer always felt elegant and enticing with gleaming white marble tile and luscious green palms and ferns, but it seemed different today. The huge white marble staircase no longer beckoned invitingly. The house was cold, almost forbidding. I shivered.

What's the matter with you this morning? I shook myself and entered the music room, which I'd searched meticulously before. White oak French doors divulged a roomful of musical treasures including a glittering golden harp and dazzling white grand piano, both of which I'd nearly dismantled in my search.

I'd grown up with stories of Margo as I helped Alma care for this enchanting home—the star's blonde beauty and sparkling blue eyes, her lovely voice, her verve and vitality. She had lavished her wealth on worthy projects in the area and was loved and revered by all who remembered her. I felt I knew this elusive woman who'd vanished mysteriously, and yet I knew nothing. Why did I think Margo held some clue to my father's whereabouts?

Standing in the center of the room, I looked for anything I'd missed. Then I heard it . . . a sound totally out of place here. I stood still, not breathing, waiting to hear it again.

The house was quiet, except for the pounding of my heart. *What was it?* Not an animal, nor did it sound like someone moving in the house. *Had I imagined it?* No. Padding softly to the window in my stocking feet, I was distressed to see the black ship still off the cove. I stood for several minutes, listening, but the strange sound was not repeated. It had been as foreign to the house as that ship was in the cove.

I'd never been frightened of being alone in this magnificent mansion. Only good things happened to me here. But now I couldn't shake the ominous feeling that shrouded me.

I moved to the ballroom through beveled glass doors etched with musical motifs, then glided across the ballroom floor, a masterpiece of white oak parquet inlaid with brass musical symbols scattered here and there.

Four sets of French doors opened onto a white marble patio in front of the house. On the opposite wall stood an immense fireplace, and above the gold-veined white marble mantle hung a haunting picture of Margo dressed in floating white chiffon, a filmy drape blowing across her shoulders.

I paused to run my fingers over the five-foot-tall gold peacock that fanned its filigreed feathers in front of the fireplace. I loved the emerald eyes. Alma assured me they were authentic, but who would put emeralds as big as my thumbnail in a fireplace decoration? Then again, Margo had spent several fortunes on this splendid house. The emeralds probably were real.

As I reached to touch them, the hair on my arms stood on end. I felt eyes watching me and I whirled around—but no one was there. *What's happening?* I'd never had these sensations when there was no apparent danger. Each time I'd experienced these warnings in the past, I'd been saved from some perilous circumstance. As a child, running through the hills with my friend Bart, I stopped just short of a nest of rattlesnakes. Premonitions prevented me from stepping into an intersection in New York when a speeding car ran a red light. I could count a dozen other times I had been forewarned of imminent danger.

What danger is here? Why can't I see it? I ran to the music room, only to find it empty. No one on the patio. I stood in the shadow of the drapes, listening. Nothing.

Allison, you're a grown woman, an expert in self-defense, and not given to fantasies.

The magic had faded from the ballroom, which I'd searched thoroughly before. Today my concentration was on the library. First I'd report last night's episode on the beach to the police, then call Mom in Athens and tell her I'd arrived safely. What else? That I'd been hearing things, that my danger antennae were tingling for no discernible reason?

Stained glass on bookshelf doors danced with light reflected from the crystal chandelier. This was no dark, shadowy library, but a bright, inviting room. Or had been. Today, even sun streaming through big windows behind cushion-covered window seats wasn't enough to dispel the gloom settling over me.

As I picked up the phone, I somehow knew there would be no dial tone. The phone was dead. *Was the line purposely cut? Should I stay and search for the clue I felt was at my fingertips, or run—but from what?*

I looked around the library. White wrought-iron staircases spiraled to the ceiling in each corner and a reading loft haloed the top of the room.

On the walls hung pictures of the nine Greek muses, goddesses of arts and sciences. I could name each one, had studied them all, and was named after one, though Mom had shortened it from Melpomena to Melanie. Melanie Allison Alexander. Soon to be Mrs. Milton J.

Hollingsworth, III. At the thought, the churning in the pit of my stomach returned with a vengeance.

Not now. I won't think of it now. I fought to suppress the familiar feelings, the old fears, and force my focus back to the business at hand.

In this room, I'd written essays, done research papers, and spent lazy hours being transported to enchanted lands. Here I began the formal study of the dozen foreign languages I'd picked up on our travels as Mom did research all over the world.

The carpeted reading loft had snug, inviting corners. I'd received my first unmistakable impression here that my father was alive. I knew . . . I KNEW he loved me; I felt his sorrow at not being with me. The feeling was so intense, so real, I reached out to touch him. He wasn't there, but the experience assured me that he was alive.

I needed some assurance now. I was torn between trepidation at ignoring my feelings of danger, and my desire to seek desperately needed answers.

My stocking feet padded softly on cold metal as I climbed the circular staircase. Cushions waited exactly as I'd left them and I sank into their hospitable softness.

I hugged the mauve velvet pillow, still tear-stained from many sessions in this corner. *Where are you, Dad? Where do you spend your days and months and years? Why do you let everyone else believe you're dead? Why did you leave me?*

That was the question that haunted me relentlessly. *Why did the men I loved always leave me?* First my father whom I'd absolutely adored, then beloved Uncle Mike, then Alma and Jim's son, Bart—my best friend, my first love. Now I could acknowledge Uncle Mike had simply died, but as a child I felt betrayed by his disappearance.

By habit, I rolled over and pressed my nose against the

window that overlooked the bay. The strange ship still brooded in the cove. My senses screamed trouble. Decision time. *Do I run—or do I stay?*

Chapter Two

I stayed. My obsession to find the connection to my father won over good sense. Suspecting the house contained more secret passages than the one I'd known about all my life, I'd measured each room against the outside dimensions of the house. Those measurements convinced me the library wall bordered on an undiscovered passage.

I felt like a character from an Agatha Christie novel as I pushed the gold musical notes adorning the wall. A section of music books swung open silently, revealing a passageway that led to Margo's closet.

As I hesitated at the entrance to the darkened passage, I heard the front door open, then slam shut. Instinctively, I turned to holler, "Who's there?", then stopped. Had the intruders returned? Voices, unfamiliar, gruff, got louder as they advanced through the ballroom and headed straight for the library!

I ducked inside the secret passage, activating the switch that closed the door, plunging me into total darkness. I knew they hadn't heard it close. Bart and I experimented many times to make sure the panels were completely silent. *Why did they come to the library?*

I stood quietly, ear pressed to the door, trying to discover who they were and what they wanted. They were directly outside the library, voices hushed. Heavy footsteps resumed. In the library. On the wrought-iron stairs next to the music case, heading straight for the passage in which I stood, terrified. *Do they know about it?*

I whirled to the other end of the passage to escape through Margo's bedroom, then stopped abruptly in the middle. Someone was in Margo's closet. I was trapped!

Think, Allison. You calculated there was another passage at this point, between the library and Margo's closet. Find it.

There were no switches or buttons, nothing on these walls. I knew. Bart and I helped Alma oil the walnut paneling. I swept my hands across the paneling, up to the ceiling, down again, searching each. *I can't find it! I'm cornered!*

Then an unmistakable impression—my father—indicating the top of the seam on the panel. I found a seam, ran my fingers upward along the smooth silky finish to a small nail that needed one more pound with a hammer. I pushed it. The wall slid open on a passage the length of the library wall, illuminated by a small, red light bulb.

How do I close it? Panic choked me. The other had closed with a mechanism in the corner. I slid my foot into the corner. No bulge. They were at the music shelf—*they know about the passage! They'd come directly to it.*

Be calm. I began in the corner, drug my foot along the baseboard until it hit something, then pressed hard with my big toe. The wall silently closed behind me just as the light from the library flowed into the darkened passage.

Did they see the panel close? I held my breath and didn't move. *Who were they? How did they know I was in the library?* They must have known—they'd come directly here. *How did they know about the secret passage?*

I crept to the end of the passage, slid down the wall, and sat on the floor. By what means could my father direct me here? This wasn't the first time he'd saved me from danger. I never received the impressions if I could handle my problem, only when I was helpless. I prided myself that wasn't often. *How does he know when I'm in danger?*

Their hands were sliding, pounding on the walls, searching for another passage.

"There's gotta be a secret room," a gravelly voice said. "The bug picked her up in the library, but not in the bedroom. She's here somewhere."

"I'll search every inch of this hallway." Another voice, not as coarse. The pounding started on the opposite wall.

"What'cha doin'?" the gravelly voice growled.

"Listenin' for hollow walls—to find the other passage." The pummeling continued.

My heart stopped beating as the thumping approached my wall. One more foot and he'd hit the hidden panel. The pounding progressed.

"Give it up, Sam," Gravel Voice commanded. "There ain't nothin' here."

The hammering ceased. *Inches more and he'd have found me.* I hugged my knees tight and dropped my head on them. I was drained!

This can't be happening! Not here. Not at home. If I were with Mom in Europe, or Asia . . . We'd had many close calls as I traveled with Mom to villages, recording folk songs, dances, stories, and legends of various cultures. We'd been threatened by witch doctors, taken captive by marauding tribes, kidnapped by a crazy Greek who'd fallen for Mom, and robbed in the big city; I expected danger from that quarter. Not in our peaceful hideaway. Not here.

I heard thumping periodically. Then the house got quiet. I waited hours, curled up as comfortably as possible, letting my mind recreate games of hide and seek as a child with Bart when I had to sit quietly for a long time until he either found me or gave up. I fished the apple from my pocket and feasted.

I was struck by a sudden thought. *How do I get out?* Then another realization shook me. This was a dead end. What was its purpose . . . unless it led to another room or passage?

I'd hardly moved for hours for fear a creaking board or bump against the wall might give me away. Now I was jolted into action.

I began in one corner on what should have been the back of Margo's closet and felt up as far as I could reach. No lumps or bumps or nails. I did the same in the other corner and came up empty handed.

My fingers performed a glissade over the satiny finish of the dark paneling. Not even a sliver. In one final sweep up the wall, my finger hit a small protuberance. I pushed it up and was rewarded by stale, musty air flowing through the opening in front of me.

A tiny landing led to a narrow, steep staircase, lit only by the glow of a small red light. To my right was Margo's bedroom. I was behind Margo's enormous walk-in closet.

But where could the stairs lead? There wasn't a third floor and I was already on the second. *Ah! The widow's walk!* Jim said it was for looks and only accessible by ladder from outside. *We'll see about that!* At the top, there was no door. Only a wall. Why would Margo put another secret panel here?

I began at the bottom of the wall, examining every inch as high as I could reach. No seams, just a single smooth piece of paneling.

This had to lead somewhere. As I leaned against the wall, a section behind me slid open and I almost fell into a little room—a secret room!

I'd expected to enter the widow's walk, not a little roomful of what . . . round, flat tins neatly stacked on shelves along one wall. A sparkling white square covered the end wall. A movie screen?

The soft red glow revealed a black sofa with a white fur throw and a desk with a typewriter. Two white overstuffed chairs completed the snug little room's inventory. The screen was puzzling, unless this was Margo's own private screening room.

I needed to get to the widow's walk. A ladder, nailed to the wall, led up to a trap door with a switch beside it. I flipped the switch, hoping the ceiling would open to the outside. It did.

The widow's walk was about eight feet square surrounded by a parapet three feet high. I stayed low so I wouldn't be silhouetted against the twilight sky.

I couldn't wait even a few minutes. Peeking over the ledge, I looked toward the ship in the bay. No lights on it. No movement anywhere. Wait. Coming up the trail from the beach were two figures, dark against the white foam of the surf below, each with a bundle thrown over their shoulders.

The men advanced directly toward the house with long confident strides. Nothing stealthy about these two. They headed straight for the front door and I heard it open, then close. What right had those men to just walk into Margo's house?

I crept slowly, silently across the floor and returned to the secret room.

A man, ruggedly handsome, with a confident air and mischievous grin gazed at me from a life-sized portrait on the last wall. I jumped in fright, flushed with goose bumps. He looked vaguely familiar, but he could wait. I turned to the baseboard where I found a switch that closed the panel, sealing me into this snug little sanctuary.

I thought of the men who had entered the house. What were they carrying? Were they moving into Margo's house? Nothing made sense.

I searched the desk, finding only a clutter of musical scores, typewritten scripts, and handwritten notes which covered a piano-shaped telephone. Under the shuffle of papers, I found a tiny, faceted crystal case with a treble clef inlaid in gold on the top. Inside on a blue velvet cushion lay a tiny gold key.

It didn't fit the desk, which wasn't locked anyway. I dropped into the chair nearest the picture, gripping the overstuffed arms as I stared into the laughing eyes of the mysterious man. Margo had never married. Was he the reason?

Suddenly I was aware my fingers were tracing a metal design on the front of the right arm of the chair. I knelt to examine it in the dim light. *A keyhole!*

Fingers trembling with excitement, I fumbled to open the crystal case and try the tiny key in the opening. With a click, the chair arm popped open. I laid open the whole top of the overstuffed arm and let it hang by its hinges while I gaped in disbelief at an array of labeled switches: foyer, music room, ballroom, library, bedroom, guest rooms 1 through 10, servants' quarters 1 through 10, kitchen, dining room, screening room, sitting room, pool, patio.

There were two rows of knobs: video and audio. A security system? Did Margo sit here and watch the goings-on in the house? The movie screen came to life as I pressed the video button labeled "Music Room," clearly displaying the whole room.

Systematically I searched each room. All were empty and quiet, except for the last room in the servants' quarters. Two men, rough-looking, dirty, and unshaven were arguing. I recognized their voices. These filthy, frightening-looking men had come within inches of finding me in the library! I shuddered with horror at what might have happened if they'd found the passage.

I gasped as they pulled the duffle bags from the closet, and from each bag, a beautiful Oriental child! The men untied the children's hands and feet and thrust a paper sack toward them, signalling to them to eat.

"He'll kill us if we lose them!" Gravel Voice shouted. "I say we tie 'em up and lock 'em back in the closet. You're too soft-hearted, Sam."

"They ain't goin' nowhere. Jack don't want 'em hurt, right? Then leave 'em loose and we'll lock 'em in." Sam nervously rubbed a large mole at the side of his nose.

Leaving the two children huddled on the bed, clinging to each other, the men walked out and locked the door. Where did they get keys to the house? There were only two sets of keys to the estate. The ones in my pocket, and Jim and Alma's. This wasn't the "breaking and entering" job I'd first thought.

Whoever they were, these children were obviously in danger from the same source as mine. I had to help them. I pushed all the buttons, scanning the house, but the two men were gone.

I climbed up to the widow's walk. The dirty duo disappeared over the cliff toward the beach, making no attempt to hide their flashlights.

I had to move quickly. Opening the panel to the passageway, I raced down the stairs, wishing I'd taken time to locate the entrance I felt sure led into Margo's closet.

How long before the two men came back? Then I had a thought that turned my stomach upside down. *The third man—the one they called Jack! What if he was still in the house?*

I assumed Margo could go directly into her closet from the secret room and not through the other passageway first. Finally, at the bottom of the first step, I found a lump in the corner. The wall in front of me slid open.

I was right! Margo's off-season closet. I raced down the winding staircase to the lower level of her bedroom, into the hall, through the grand foyer and down the other hall to room 10. My fumbling fingers could hardly get the key in the door.

As I opened the door, four big dark eyes looked up in fear—then surprise.

"I won't hurt you. Come with me and I'll hide you." The children didn't move.

"I came to help. Please hurry."

They don't speak English; they don't understand me. I knelt by the bed and touched the frightened little girl's hand. Softly I whispered, first in Mandarin, then Japanese, "I won't hurt you. I want to help. We must go—now, before those bad men come back."

The boy was holding his sister's hands; he put them in mine and jumped off the bed. I scooped the little girl into my arms, blanket, lunch sack, and all.

We flew down the dark hall with my little bundle clinging tightly to my neck and the boy grasping my shirttail. Before leaving the safety of the kitchen, we paused, listening, but the house was hushed and still.

At the corner by the sitting room, I paused briefly before entering the foyer. *If there's no light on, the men aren't here, right?*

We dashed into the foyer. I stopped dead in my tracks. Footsteps clicked on the marble floor in the very hall we were approaching. I grabbed at Big Brother but he was one step ahead of me. We wheeled and raced up the marble stairs, rounding the first curve as the clicks reached the foyer and the lower light flipped on.

He didn't move—no clicks or noise at all. *Had he heard us?*

Big Brother snuggled against me, but remained poised for flight. Little Sister's strong legs were wrapped around my waist so I couldn't have shaken her loose if I tried.

Click. Click. Metal tips on marble. He moved up two steps and stopped. Click. Click. Back down the stairs and across the foyer toward the kitchen corridor.

The foyer went dark and I heard the metal taps click down the hall. Silently we moved again, around the last curve of the spiral, into the blessedly dark upstairs hall to Margo's room. I cracked the door and listened, opened it just enough to slip through with Big Brother at my side.

Relief swept through me as I closed the panel, securing us in my secret room sanctuary.

I collapsed in the chair, loosened Little Sister's death grip from around my neck and held her head against me, stroking her hair. Big Brother gazed around the room in awe, examining his new surroundings.

As I flipped the first switch lighting the monitor, Little Sister jumped. Big Brother was obviously delighted. I searched each room, but the house was empty and quiet. Where was Jack, or whoever he was? There were no monitors in the halls. He could be patrolling anywhere, or he could have gone back to the ship.

How long will we have to stay here? Can we get out without being seen? Where can I take my two little charges? What have

I gotten us into? Will we be trapped here and die of starvation? I groaned. Little Sister wasn't happy about being disturbed. Gently I laid her on the sofa and covered her with the blanket. She curled up and was soon asleep.

Big Brother heard my stomach growl and, retrieving the sack from under the blanket, offered me a banana. I thanked him, grateful I'd scooped up the sack with blanket and child.

I examined the contents of their lunch sack—a couple of apples and bananas, granola bars, and yogurt. At least it wasn't a cold hamburger and greasy fries. *This should keep us from starving until I could figure out what to do,* I thought.

I was exhausted, emotionally and physically. Big Brother fought valiantly to stay awake. I guided him gently to the other end of the sofa. He flashed a smile and gave me a thumbs-up sign. I kissed his forehead, tucking the blanket around him.

The fur throw would be my security blanket tonight. I snuggled down in the arm chair, leaving the monitor on the foyer and the volume turned up slightly to alert me to anyone entering the house.

I woke sometime later temporarily disoriented. Movement on the monitor caught my eye. A casually but neatly-dressed man with an authoritative air about him paced the foyer.

He waited—impatiently—for someone. His pacing quickened. Turning up the sound on the monitor, I heard the click of metal taps. *The third man! Jack—the one who instilled fear into the gruesome, grimy twosome.*

The front door opened and Gravel Voice stepped hesitantly into the foyer.

"You wanted to talk to me?" he growled, but his voice was less belligerent than it had been yesterday with Sam.

"Where are the children?" Jack demanded, his voice low

and controlled. "I told you to take good care of them. We can't ransom damaged goods."

"I put 'em in an upstairs bedroom so they'd be comfortable, like I told ya."

That was more lie than truth. Sam was the one who insisted they not be shackled and locked up.

"The kids are not in a bedroom, nor anywhere else in this house. I've looked. Where are they?"

With intense interest, I watched the scene play out until Jack ordered Tony to bring the ship's crew to the house to search for the missing children. What if they found us? I'd stumbled upon the hidden passageways and the secret room. What was to stop them from doing the same? *We have to leave! But where can we go?*

Chapter Three

The General! The best hiding place of all and no one would think of looking for us there. When I was sure they were gone, I roused Big Brother and picked up Little Sister, wrapping the blanket securely around her.

"You take this," I indicated, thrusting the lunch sack at Big Brother. "We have to leave now." I scanned the house one last time on the monitor, then opened the panel in the wall with mixed feelings about leaving our hideaway.

As my stocking feet hit the damp cold of the front steps, I remembered my shoes by the front door and quickly slipped them on, grateful the intruders hadn't taken them. Suddenly a light flashed up the trail from the beach. Ducking behind the shrubs and pressing close to the wall, we made it around the southwest corner of the house before the light topped the cliff.

Too soon we reached the far end of the house and had to leave the protection of the shrubs. Our safety now would depend on speed, luck, and the cover of pre-dawn darkness.

From the back of the house, beginning almost immediately at the guest room verandas, the grounds sloped downhill. Margo hadn't tampered with the natural beauty of the terrain, except to plant grass between towering Spanish oaks that spread twisted branches like giant umbrellas over huge rock formations.

It was toward the most impressive of these trees that we now made our way, racing across an open space of lawn to the nearest cluster of rocks.

Pale streaks of light illuminated the sky. Our cover of darkness was fading; our saving grace was the morning mist moving in off the Pacific Ocean. We raced from one clump of trees to the next, stopping briefly at the grove to catch our breath.

I pointed to a huge tree silhouetted against the first rays of day. "We're going way over there on the hill." Could Big Brother understand?

We made another wild dash for cover behind the next bunch of rocks and trees. As we reached it, I heard shouts from the house. Had they seen us before the mist swallowed us? If we'd been spotted, it was only a matter of minutes before they'd be here. I trembled to think what would happen if we were caught.

The mist was always heaviest by the creek, so I knew we were near it when I could no longer see shapes around me. I slowed to a quick walk until I heard water rushing over rocks in the creek bed straight ahead.

In midsummer, I could cross the creek almost anywhere, and by fall a tiny trickle, if that, remained. But this was still early spring and the creek was a tumble of wildly rushing water that could only be crossed at the bridge. To my right or left? I chanced we'd stayed in a fairly straight line from the rocks to the creek, and turned right.

Through the mist a lovely curve arched over the water, just like a scene from *Madame Butterfly*, complete with weeping willows lining the creek. The creek was the outer limit of the manicured grass and from there, an open meadow stretched toward a steep, rock-strewn hillside.

I could barely see the giant tree through the mist, but I knew it was there. I sensed it before I saw it. Its massive power reached out to draw me in. We quickly crossed the open meadow, peering into the gray fog that shrouded us. I saw no one, felt no presence, but my apprehension didn't leave me until I was safely in the shadow of the mammoth trunk.

I stepped onto the lowest branch, big as a tree itself, that angled off low enough for a child to climb on before it began its stretch toward the sky. Big Brother's face lit up as he realized we were going to hide in the tree and he climbed easily into the nest, reaching down to pull Little Sister in as I boosted her.

I hugged the rough, silver-gray bark of this friendly giant to keep my wildly beating heart from leaping from my breast. How many times my friend had comforted, cradled, hid me.

I was five the first time I saw it, looming as large as the giant redwood they called General Sherman, so I named it "the General."

It became one of my favorite spots, and I still fit into it, like a hand sliding into a comfortable old glove. Four branches, each angling in a different direction, created a cozy nest which had been my refuge for years. We'd barely settled into our hiding place when I heard voices. We had been followed!

They were still some distance. I couldn't hear what they were saying, but I guessed they were near the bridge. Any minute the sun would peek over the hills, creating enough light to see where the mist wasn't obscuring everything.

It was suddenly quiet. I strained to hear, not daring to

breathe. Had they gone back? They wouldn't give up that easily.

"Yo! Tony! Sam! Meet me at the bridge. There wasn't anything out here. Sam must have been hallucinating. Those kids are in the house somewhere." It was Jack.

I heard snatches of muttering and grumbling and footsteps over the bridge. Then all was quiet. Slowly my racing heartbeat returned to normal and I breathed again.

We settled into the protecting embrace of the tree. I laughed to myself. Embrace comes from the Latin *in-bracchium*—literally, "to hold in one's arms." The General was certainly doing that. How long could we stay here? Actually, the question was, how long would we *have* to stay?

A whispered "Wow!" escaped Big Brother. I looked sharply at him. He grinned sheepishly. "We thank you, kind lady, for rescuing us."

"Okay, guys, how about some answers? Who are you? Where did you come from? How did you learn English? Why didn't you tell me you could understand me?"

"You may call me Boomer. This is my sister, Sunny. We were kidnapped from our home in Bangkok by those men. We learned your language from our governess. I did not speak until I knew if you were a friend. Now what shall we do?" He folded his arms imperiously, leaned back against the tree, and smiled broadly.

I eyed the two with amazement. This was just an adventure to them—at least to Boomer. He didn't seem the least bit worried. That was encouraging.

"How about some breakfast?" I opened the sack. *When all else fails, eat.* I started thinking ahead to what a long day it would be without water. "If you eat the yogurt now, I'll fill the empty containers from the creek so we won't get thirsty." Boomer nodded in agreement and he and Sunny finished off the yogurt, scraping up every last bit.

Sunny smiled shyly at me. "I was much more hungry than I thought." Her lovely olive cheeks dimpled as she handed me the slicked-clean container.

A tiny breeze wafted the mist here and there as I scooped two cups full of sparkling water and returned to the safety of the General. We perched the cups on a branch where they wouldn't be spilled and settled down to get acquainted.

"What is your name, pretty lady?" Sunny shyly asked.

"Melanie Allison Alexander, but you can call me Alli."

"Melanie—Allison—Alexander." She practiced until her pronunciation was perfect. Her voice was soft and sweet with a sing-song quality. "What does it mean? Miss McKenzie said my name means bright and shiny."

"Melanie is from Melpomena, Greek muse of tragedy. It means black. Allison means 'light.' Alexander is 'helper of men,' which, I'm told, my father was."

My father. My greatest mystery. Where is he? Does he have another family somewhere? No. That didn't ring true. What does he spend his time doing? Most of all, why did he leave me?

A tug at my sleeve roused me from musing. "My name is not really Boomer, but Miss McKenzie thought my given name was too long. I am known as Bhumibol in my father's house."

"I think Boomer fits you perfectly. Tell me about Miss McKenzie."

"My father hired her to be our tutor so we could learn to speak your language fluently."

"Do you know the names of the men who brought you here?"

"One is Tony. He is bad-tempered and mean. Sam is nicer, but afraid of Tony. Jack is the boss-man. He has been good to us. The men are respectful of him. They fear him.

Another is Bart."

"Bart!"

"He is very tall and younger than the others with hair that is almost white and very, very blue eyes."

"He's cute," giggled Sunny. "He gave me his dessert every night."

Could this be my Bart? A member of this gang? It had to be! There couldn't possibly be two very tall, white-blond, blue-eyed Barts in this part of the world. Why here? Why now? I hadn't seen or heard from Bart for years. I couldn't accept the fact that Bart was a kidnapper. He'd been so gentle, watching over me as we romped through rocks and trees and over golden hills. Either this wasn't my Bart, or he'd changed drastically. That could explain why he'd dropped out of my life suddenly.

"Miss Alli. Where are your thoughts taking you? It must be far away."

"Sorry, Boomer. It was—and many years ago. Would you like to see where I spent my childhood?"

"Can we go there now?"

"We don't have to move. See that pile of rocks? That was one of my favorite hiding places. My best friend lived near here and we'd play hide and seek all day. There's a hole between the trees in front of the rocks where he never found me.

"See where the creek disappears? That's a waterfall. Not a big one, about ten feet high. I discovered a cave behind the waterfall. It's a great place to spend a hot afternoon—damp, but nice and cool.

"There are two ponds below that little hill. The first is fed by the waterfall, the second by water from the first pond cascading over big boulders. They were made for a movie Margo filmed here."

"Who is Margo?" Boomer asked.

"Margo was a famous movie star who owns the house we were in and all the land as far as you can see. She designed the house, complete with secret rooms and passages, then disappeared. Margo vowed she'd return and wanted everything kept ready for her. Mom and I moved here to manage the estate when I was five and we've lived here ever since."

Sunny was watching me intently.

"Where is your mother now, Miss Alli?"

Did I detect homesickness in that query? Why not? She was such a little girl.

I looked at my watch. "Probably at the Archeological Museum in Athens. She'll go to dinner with friends at her favorite *taverna,* the Kostoyannis, then return to her villa to study the lectures she'll give this week. Tomorrow she'll visit a dig or spend time in the villages persuading the grandmothers to tell their stories."

"Why is your mother there and you are here? Did someone steal you away, too?" Sunny asked, looking more solemn by the minute.

"No, sweetheart. She travels to Greece with her work. I work in New York. No one stole me away." *At least, not yet.*

My narrative was interrupted by impressions from the house. I sensed chaos—and shots. What was happening? Icy fingers of fear gripped my heart as I thought of Bart with those cruel men. But if he was one of them. . . .

I broke out in a cold sweat and began shivering all over, though the morning had turned warm. I had a sudden impression of Dad—that he was here—that he was hurt. I sensed the ballroom, rather than seeing it, and was aware of a tremendous pain in my heart. Closing my eyes, I saw a pool of blood, spreading over the parquet floor, seeping into the crevices of a gold bass cleft.

"No!" I cried out loud. Tears squeezed from beneath my tightly clenched eyelids. I felt a sensation of falling, down, down.

"Alli! Miss Alli! Are you all right? Please look at me."

I lost whatever communication was coming to me from the house, and I opened my eyes to find two very frightened children staring at me. Tears streamed down Sunny's face as she wiped away her tears with one hand and mine with another. I hadn't felt her hand on my face. I pulled her to me.

"It's okay, Sunny, I'm all right. I just had a . . . waking nightmare. I didn't mean to frighten you."

Boomer watched me with a skeptical look. "I'm fine, Boomer, really I am. Have you ever had a nightmare?"

He nodded.

"That's what happened to me." It certainly wasn't a lie. In every way, it was a nightmare.

"None of us got much sleep last night. We don't know how long we'll have to stay here, or what we'll have to do when it's time to go, so we'd better get some rest. We'll need to think clearly and have lots of energy to escape. Sunny, you snuggle down here. Boomer, you can use my sweater for a pillow."

We settled back and almost immediately the children were asleep. *If I could close my mind as easily as I closed my eyes!* Over and over I reviewed the feelings and impressions I'd experienced. What did it mean? I knew Dad was here and he was hurt. Had he sent those messages to me about the ballroom and his pain? They were like other unmistakable impressions I'd had from him, except before it had been for my safety. *Was it now for his?*

Roused from my thoughts by shouting from the house, I strained to see what was going on. On the veranda of the guest quarters, I could see figures looking over the lawns toward us, yelling and pointing. Shifting slightly, I saw two men running from the house, searching each rock formation, even looking in the trees.

They worked their way methodically toward the creek. My heart rate spiraled as they got closer. Would they cross the creek? If they did, the General was the logical place to look. I was terrified. What would they do to me for taking Boomer and Sunny? What would they do to the children?

These were different men—not Tony, Sam, or Jack. They stopped, looked under the bridge, leaned against it as they scanned the meadow on this side of the creek. I held my breath. They looked directly at the General—at us.

Finally they appeared satisfied no one was out here. One walked to the creek and removed his hat to wipe his brow with his sleeve. Bart! My heart did a flip-flop. He knelt, drank from the creek, cupping the water in his hands as we'd done so many times as kids. He stared steadily at the General. The other man called to him. Bart gave an almost imperceptible salute with two fingers in our direction, then got up and headed back up the hill with his companion.

He did know! Why didn't he betray us? Was he on my side? Then why was he with these vile, evil men? How involved was he with the kidnappers? What were they doing at Margo's? Why had I felt fifteen again when I recognized him?

Suddenly the hurt and the pain knifed through me that I'd felt when he disappeared and I realized I'd been abandoned again. *Not now!*

I tried to contact Dad, to establish some kind of link—even an impression like I'd received before. Where was he? He'd been shot. How badly was he hurt? I wouldn't consider the possibility he was dead, expelling the thought from my mind.

In dismay, I watched Bart and the other man enter our cottage. I'd locked the door when I left the house. Had Bart remembered where the hidden key was? Would he use it with the enemy by his side? Or was he the enemy?

At length they reappeared, crossing the lawn to the big house. When all was quiet, I lay back against the tree and tried to relax.

Dad, where are you? Please talk to me. Are you okay? However you communicated with me before, do it again. I know you're here and hurt. How can I help you? He must be alive! But my mind kept saying things my heart didn't want to hear.

Chapter Four

I awoke to Sunny's gentle shaking. "Miss Alli, I have a need." She squirmed uncomfortably. I motioned to not disturb Boomer and slid down the back of the tree, helping Sunny down. We were careful to keep the tree squarely between us and the house.

When the deed was done, I stretched my arms to the pure blue spring sky. This was not how I expected to spend my time on the estate. I longed to run to the top of the hill and clear the kinks from my muscles and the cobwebs from my mind. And to wake from this nightmare.

Year after year I felt the assurance that not only would I find my father, but also that the link to him was on the estate. Now he was here, physically. But where? Why didn't he show himself? How could I find him? How badly was he hurt? There were so many questions!

Sunny picked a bouquet of the wild flowers that brightened the meadow and hillside this time of year—vividly orange California poppies, blue lupine, exquisitely colored Davy gilia, and little white tidytips. She presented me with her gathered treasures and we climbed back into our sanctuary—or was it our prison?

Bart and I had gathered armfuls of these brilliant blossoms every spring for our mothers, and every year they were wilted before we got them delivered. He was my knight in shining armor, the big brother I never had, the hero I idolized, and though he was four years older than me, Bart had been my best friend. I couldn't believe he was part of this gang of kidnappers . . . and murderers? My heart ached at the thought.

What of Dad? Tears welled in my eyes as I considered how close I finally felt to solving the mysteries of my past. *What if, before I could get to him, he . . .* I couldn't say it. I couldn't even think it.

Dear God. Please don't let my dad be dead.

"Miss Alli, I am very hungry. May I please have something to eat?" Sunny asked.

"Of course, sweetheart. How about a granola bar? Do you have these in Thailand?"

"I saw them on television. My father says we are to learn what American children learn, so we watch programs from America. You have a nice country, but I want to go home." Tears welled up in Sunny's eyes and spilled down her cheeks. I held her close, not knowing how to comfort her.

Our conversation awakened Boomer and he joined Sunny in polishing off the last morsel of food. There were still the things I'd brought with me from the country store and left on the counter in the cottage. I'd sneak back after dark and retrieve them. We passed time telling stories and fairy tales.

My spirits lifted a little with the possibility that the men hadn't found the keys to my car and we could get away. *But can I leave without knowing about Dad? And if I did leave, where could I take the children? Without Dad . . .*

How final it sounded. How empty. It didn't matter that I'd grown up without him, physically. I'd felt his influence—

and his love—throughout my life. He would, I knew, someday come back into my life.

As the sun sank lower, the night breezes from the ocean set the wildflowers waving and us shivering. I was glad for my sweater and the blanket for the children. We snuggled closer. It would be an uncomfortable night without extra blankets. When it was dark, I'd go to the house.

I was so wrapped up in my thoughts that I scarcely noticed Boomer and Sunny talking quietly. When Boomer saw they had my attention, he reached for a satin pouch Sunny carried around her neck.

"Miss Alli, we need to give this to you for safekeeping. If they catch us, they will find it. These could be used to buy our freedom." Boomer handed me the pouch. I gasped as I opened it. A dozen unset diamonds bigger than my thumbnail and a handful of other precious stones rattled loosely in the velvet pouch. One huge emerald surrounded by diamonds gleamed in a most magnificent setting.

"Boomer, where did you get these? They're worth a fortune!"

"When Tony and Sam took us from our father's house, they also took the jewels. We swoped them back as they slept." He looked at me questioningly.

"You mean swiped. You swiped them back."

"Yes. Tony suspects we have them and has been very angry with us. He would have hurt us but Jack stopped him. We hid them on the ship, and brought them with us. But they will help us only if Tony does not find them."

"What do you want me to do with them?"

"Please put them in a safe place where they cannot be found."

I tucked the bag of jewels into my pocket. If I could get back into the big house, I knew the perfect spot.

"Boomer, your family must be very wealthy. Is that why you and Sunny were taken from your parents' house?"

With a slight bow of his head, Boomer formally introduced himself. "I am firstborn grandson of His Majesty, Bhumibol Adjulyadej, the ninth King of Thailand in the Chakri Dynasty. Someday I will be king. There are certain factions that do not like a monarchy and wish to take over power in our government, much like your American Revolution," he added with a mischievous grin.

Then more seriously, he continued. "My sister and I were with Miss McKenzie and her family, preparing to attend a celebration, but Tony and Sam took us before we could go."

"Boomer, I haven't read anything. . . ."

"No, Miss Alli." Boomer interrupted. "My family would not announce we have been taken. They would hope to return us before our next appearance to the public. We would not be seen again until the birthday of Her Majesty, the Queen, on August 12. We must be returned to my father's house by that time."

I couldn't believe what I was hearing. Boomer had matter-of-factly told me he was heir to the Thai throne and in the following breath that they needed to be returned before the next royal holiday so no one would know they'd been kidnapped. Never mind that he had given me a small fortune in family jewels. I had major problems on my hands. Instead of two ordinary children to return to a foreign country, I had a prince, a princess, and a treasure!

Sunny shivered and snuggled closer to me. I must go for more blankets. Or should I move the children from the estate? No—I needed to stay near my father. I refused to think of the possibility I wouldn't soon find him—or that it might be too late when I did. But now, we needed warm blankets and something more to eat.

"Here, Sunny. Here's my sweater, and you two wrap up in the blanket. As soon as it's dark, I'll go to the cottage for blankets and whatever I can find to eat. Snuggle close to me and we'll be warm."

Cuddling together, we were temporarily more comfortable. My mind was racing. I couldn't believe I had the heir to the throne of Thailand and his royal sister curled up beside me. It was a good thing their law had been changed which said no commoner could touch a royal personage. I could be beheaded for this! One of the Thai queens had drowned while several servants looked helplessly on. It was forbidden to touch a royal person and they had not dared disobey the law, even to save their queen!

Leaning back against the tree, I closed my eyes. My thoughts turned suddenly with a strange urgency to Mom. *I must warn her of danger.* The impression was so strong I couldn't sit one minute longer, even to wait for the safety of darkness.

"I'm going now to hide your jewels and get food and blankets. Stay here." I slipped down the back of the tree and checked toward the house. No lights. No sign of anyone. The sense of urgency overcame even my great fear of being caught.

Keeping low and behind rocks and trees, I was at the cottage in a matter of minutes. My first priority was to hide the jewels but to do that I needed tape. Quietly I tried the door knob. Unlocked. Pushing the door open just far enough to reach into the first drawer of the roll-top desk, I grabbed the tape and dashed across the lawn to the mansion, keeping in the shadows wherever possible, watching for guards as I ran.

I listened for sounds in the house before I proceeded. All seemed deathly still. *Bad thought!* I slipped in a side door, down the hall to Margo's room, and crept up the circular staircase to her second floor. It was no little feat of dexterity, but I managed to place the jewels, imitating a movie I'd seen. *Thanks, Mr. Hitchcock!*

Again my thoughts turned to Mom with a surge of urgency. I must warn her of danger, though I didn't know exactly what. How? The piano-shaped telephone! I hadn't tried it while I was in the secret room. Was it a private line? One only Margo had used? Jim and Alma were to keep everything working. Even a hidden telephone? If this line came in from a different direction, a different hookup, the gang might have missed it when they cut the other lines.

It took only seconds to travel from Margo's room to the secret room. A dial tone! *Thank you, God, for small blessings!*

I dialed the number of the villa in Athens, but there was no answer. *Please, Mom, be there,* I pleaded. I let the phone ring and ring, endlessly, and finally, Maria, Mom's maid, answered.

"Maria, I must talk to Mom. Is she there?" I blurted in Greek. "Please give her this message the minute she comes in. It's very important! There's danger! Do you understand? *Kindinos!* She's to go to the grandmothers, to Sybil, and wait. Did you get that? *Efcharisto, Maria. Kali Andamosi."*

As I hung up, Maria was still firing questions at me that I couldn't answer. I visualized her with the phone in one hand and the other waving in the air. "Thank you and good-bye? Thank you and good-bye!" she would be repeating in Greek. I knew no more than I'd just told her, and I had more questions than she did.

Who were "the grandmothers"? Would my mother know what the message meant? Who was Sybil? It meant prophetess in Greek. Was one of the grandmothers a prophetess? But the greatest question in my mind was, how did I know all this? The only possible answer comforted me.

It meant Dad was still alive, sending a message to Mom through me.

I'd hidden the colored stones in Margo's bedroom. The diamonds needed to be in the library. Reluctantly I left the safety of the secret room. Only the knowledge the children needed me back as soon as possible with food and blankets could make me leave at all. In no time I'd stashed the diamonds, and, that part of my mission easily accomplished, I turned my attention to food and blankets.

Carefully I backtracked across the lawn to our cottage. I wished I'd checked to see if Mom left any food for me. I wouldn't dare use a light, just grab what I'd left on the table, the blankets, and beat a hasty retreat to the General where Sunny and Boomer would be waiting, cold, worried, and impatient.

Slipping in the door I'd left ajar, I headed immediately for my bedroom to strip the blankets from my bed. I froze as my foot touched the bottom stair. Had I heard someone, something, in the house, or were my ears and nerves playing tricks on me? I didn't move—couldn't move. For what seemed an eternity, I stood motionless, listening, before I dared take one more step, then another.

In the movies, the center of the step creaked, so I hugged the wall. It took forever to reach the top. I crossed the landing and crept into my bedroom.

As I peeled the blankets from my bed, the hair stood up on the back of my neck. I knew without turning around that someone was standing directly behind me. I rolled onto the bed and off the other side and was at the open balcony door before I heard my pursuer clear the bed.

I threw the blankets over the balcony and started after them. One leg was all I got over the railing before strong arms grabbed me from behind and pulled me back. A rough hand covered my mouth, cutting short the scream forming in my throat.

"Hi, Princess," a familiar voice whispered in my ear. "It's your knight in slightly tarnished armor, returned home again."

"Bart!" I stopped struggling and hung limply against him. He held me so tight my feet couldn't reach the floor.

"Here we are—where dreams are spun out of golden moonbeams and sewed together with the silver threads of stars." I gasped in astonishment that he remembered the silly prattling of a love-struck teenager so many years ago.

"What's that noise up there?" a voice called from downstairs. Gravel Voice! I stiffened and Bart tightened his grip on my mouth, arms, and waist.

"Our little mouse came for the cheese and got caught in the trap," Bart called back, "just as I said she would."

I felt sick. Once again I'd been betrayed by the only other man I'd ever loved as much as my father. First he had deserted me, then I'd been caught because Bart knew me so well he could predict where I'd go and what I'd do. I blinked back tears.

With his mouth still against my ear, he started to whisper something, but I didn't want to hear. I tried to bite his hand, kick his legs, wriggle out of his ever-tightening hold on me—anything before Gravel Voice made it up the stairs. It didn't work. Tony flipped the light on as he stormed into the bedroom waving a wicked-looking knife.

"Let's see who's caused all this trouble and fouled up my plans." He growled menacingly as he advanced toward us. Bart swung me around out of his reach.

"You know the plan. She's all mine and if you lay a finger on her, I'll kill you. Nothing works without her and she has to be in picture-perfect condition, so back off NOW!"

The two of them glared at each other over my head and Gravel Voice finally muttered an oath, cursing both of us.

"Where'd you hide them kids?" he snapped, brandishing the knife in my direction. "I wanna know right now."

Bart dropped his hand to his jacket pocket and it came up filled with a gun.

"Not a word," he hissed in my ear. He needn't have worried. I was tongue-tied with fear.

"Back off, Tony, or I'll cut you out of your share right now. If you want to live to spend a penny, stay away from her. I'll do the interrogating. Get back to the ship where you're supposed to be."

Tony snarled and sputtered, but finally stormed down the stairs and out the front door. I felt giddy with relief when he was gone. I was, by turns, furious with Bart at his treatment of me, grateful to him for saving me from Tony, and crushed at his betrayal of our friendship.

"Will you please let go of me and tell me what this is all about? What plan? What part do I play? And what do you mean, I'm yours? Bart, what happened today? What was all the shooting about?"

Bart sagged enough at my final questions to let me slip out of his arms and face him. But he turned quickly away.

"Bart, look at me. What's going on? Are you part of this gang of kidnappers? What happened to you when you disappeared from the earth? Where have you been? Talk to me!"

Before he could answer, we heard something downstairs—in the kitchen and under the balcony at the same time. In one smooth motion, Bart turned off the light with the hand that still held the gun and lifted me toward the door.

"Hush," he whispered, moving us effortlessly to the balcony. Two small shadows loaded with blankets disappeared into the night. I held my breath. At least they wouldn't be cold and hungry . . . if only Bart hadn't seen them.

"Were they supposed to follow you or stay put until you got back?" Bart asked quietly.

My heart sank. "What will you do to them?"

"Nothing now. They'll be safe from Tony in the General and when we need them, we'll know where to find them."

I was glad it was dark. I didn't want to see the coldness in his eyes that I heard in his voice.

"What happens now, Bart? Am I your prisoner?"

"Now, little princess, you're going to bed to get your beauty sleep. We have a long, exciting day tomorrow and you must look your best for the photographer. I'll stand guard in case Tony gets any bright ideas about forcing the whereabouts of the children from you. I think he's gone back to the ship, but I'll be here in the event he didn't."

"Sleep? I couldn't sleep if my life depended on it."

"Clever choice of words, Princess. Your life will depend on how well you follow orders the next few days. I advise you to stick to me like glue. Tony's crazy and dangerous. Jack. . . ."

"Who's Jack? What happened today?"

"Allison . . . ," he stopped.

"Well?" I waited for Bart's answer. He took so long I was afraid he'd gone to sleep.

"Jack was shot." He spoke softly, his voice filled with emotion.

"And? What's unusual about scum like these blowing each other away?"

"Go to sleep. We'll talk about it in the morning."

"No. We'll talk about it now."

Suddenly I felt like someone had hit me in the stomach. Waves of nausea swept over me. The realization hit me with such force that I grabbed the edge of my bed to keep from passing out on the spot.

"Jack is my father."

Chapter Five

It wasn't a question. It was a fact. The knowledge made me sick—to come so close to finding him, then have it be this way.

"Yes."

"Yes? Is that all you have to say? I know something terrible happened to him. I heard a shot, felt a pain in my heart, saw a pool of blood. Please talk to me."

"Jack, your dad, ordered Tony back to the ship, fearful Tony would find you and the children. Tony got mean, accused us of trying to get the jewels and ransom for ourselves, and turned on your dad. Before we knew what was happening, Tony pulled his gun and shot Jack. Sam and I grabbed Tony, but by the time we'd taken the gun away and calmed him down, Jack had disappeared. I honestly don't know what happened to him. I searched everywhere. I know he was hurt bad. I'm sorry, Alli. I figure he must have headed for a doctor."

"In what? My car was the only one here. It's still here. If he was hurt badly, how could he have gone far?"

"You still ask questions in multiples. I've never met anyone who asks so many questions without waiting for answers! We won't solve this puzzle tonight and I've told you everything I know. I'll put your chaise lounge against the door facing the balcony. If Tony tries anything, I'll be ready. Please, no more questions."

My mind was awhirl with questions! And I had answers to none of them.

"How did you find out Jack was my father? How long have you known? Where has he been? He's not really a . . ." No, I couldn't believe that, no matter how it looked.

"Allison, go to sleep. It's been a long day."

"What about the children?"

"Boomer's a real trouper and Sunny isn't exactly a china doll. Notice they didn't rely on you to bring the blankets and food. They can take care of themselves, with a little help here and there. Good night."

I stretched out on my bed and tried to get comfortable. In the dark, only a few feet from Bart, I was so close I could hear him breathing. I longed to reach out and touch his hand. More than that, I wanted him to hold me and tell me everything was going to be all right. That we'd find Dad in time.

"One more question," I said quietly. "Are you friend . . . or foe?"

Again he was silent for a long time.

"You must do what you're told, Allison. Please don't say anymore."

The stress returned to his voice. I'd ask no more questions. Wait a minute! Photographer? Town?

"Bart . . .?"

"No, Allison. Go to sleep!"

My body was still. My mind was racing. Where was Dad? How badly hurt was he? I concentrated on reaching out to him, hoping to receive another impression, some verification that he was okay.

Suddenly I was chilled and felt a dampness surround me. I shivered and the movement brought a sensation of pain in my shoulder.

Dad! Can you hear me? I know you're hurt. Where are you? Nothing. Even the bone-chilling dampness disappeared. I concentrated again, straining to reach him. *Dad, where are you? How can I help you?*

The chilling damp feeling returned. Wherever he was, it was wet and cold.

"Kindinos . . ." faintly. *Danger.* It wasn't words; it was an impression. A thought transference? Did Dad speak Greek? *"Warn Margaret . . . hide. Don't let them find her."*

It was like a voice with the wind blowing part of the sound away, fading in and out and hearing only a portion of it . . . as though he was delirious.

Suddenly he was gone. Maybe he'd reached the caves at the bottom of the cliffs. That was cold and damp—and filled with water when the tide came in! I had to go to him! I listened to Bart's deep breathing. Was he asleep? Trying to not make a sound, I inched one foot off the bed and touched the floor, then the other. If I could just get to the balcony, the door was still open and I could go down the tree. I raised my head off the pillow.

"Don't try it." His quiet voice was like cold steel against bare skin. "I don't want to tie you in bed. We may have to move quickly if Tony comes back."

"I've got to find Dad. He needs help. What if he made it to the caves and gets trapped when the tide comes in? Help me," I pleaded softly.

"I thought of that and looked this afternoon. He's not there."

How could he be so cold, to sit there and let Dad die?

Was it simply one less to divide the ransom with? I was furious. How much he'd changed from my kind and gentle Bart. I marched defiantly to the balcony. He couldn't order me around. I didn't hear him behind me but as I reached the door he scooped me in his arms and tossed me back on the bed.

"Don't try that again. Go to sleep." His voice was hard, final.

I'll admit I was exhausted. I would never have admitted, though, that it was comforting to have Bart close enough to touch, even if I didn't know whether he was friend or foe.

* *

The morning sun filtered through the pine trees and softly kissed me good morning. By the time I was awake enough to remember I wasn't alone, Bart seemed to be just waking, too.

"Mornin', Princess," he smiled. "Thought you were going to sleep all day! I'll bet you'd like a hot shower and change of clothes before breakfast. Be my guest. Just don't lock the bathroom door and go out the window. Tony's waiting downstairs, hoping you'll try it!" While he talked, he went through my closet and my suitcase.

"What are you doing with my clothes?"

"Ouch! Not even a 'good morning' for me? I'm picking out your clothes for today—something chic, in red. That's one of your best colors, don't you think? I always liked you in red—or emerald green to match your eyes. Here, this is perfect. Shall I run your shower for you?"

For once in my life, I was speechless! After the stony seriousness of last night, Bart was animated and friendly. This was the Bart I'd known . . . *and loved,* I was about to add. I needed some serious reflecting on my feelings. Then again, what did it matter how I felt about him? I was engaged to be married to a respectable, gentle man.

I still blush remembering when Bart caught me sketching my wedding dress. He was so cavalier, knowing he was the groom, and he had solemnly promised he'd wait for me to grow up. I saw him frequently until our graduations, his from college, mine from high school. He constantly teased me about not falling for anyone else so he could marry me, even proposed, I thought, the last time I'd seen him. Then he disappeared from my life without a word. It had been five years since I'd seen or heard from him, during which time I'd been unable to maintain a relationship with anyone—until Milton. My relationship with Milton was not romantic, but I felt safe with him.

Now, as hot water poured over me, I realized with a jolt that each time a relationship progressed to the point of seriousness, I backed away . . . in fear of being deserted again. Until this minute, I hadn't realized that I'd compared my suitors to Bart! None could hold a candle to him.

That realization was as much of a shock as the cold water that came over the top of the shower!

"Thirty minutes is long enough in there. Hurry up! We have things to do, places to go, and people to see, as the saying goes."

Bart stepped discreetly onto the balcony and surveyed the branches of the huge fir trees while I dressed. I towel-dried my black hair, flipped it upside down, and ran a comb through it. Natural curl was either a blessing or a curse. Today it was a blessing.

As I did one last mirror check, Bart came in and stood behind me. Our eyes met in the mirror. The look of pure tenderness I saw there was replaced quickly by an expression I couldn't read. Trepidation, pain, apprehension? He came closer. I couldn't move or breath. He pulled my hair back and softly kissed my neck. My knees turned to jelly and I grabbed the back of the chair to hold me up.

I turned to face him. The emotion of the moment was unbearable. I'd only read about this, never experienced it. My whole being was on fire. Bart's blue eyes seemed to be memorizing every feature of my face while his fingertip softly traced the outline of my cheek and nose and touched my lips. Then he looked into my eyes. The love I saw there melted me. It ignited desire I never thought I'd feel. I ached to have him hold me. I wanted to tell him I'd never loved anyone else . . . I belonged to him forever.

"Allison," he began softly, "I . . ."

The magic was interrupted by loud banging on the door. The mood was shattered, and Bart was suddenly cold and all business.

"Open this door before I break it down," Tony demanded.

"Hold your horses, Tony. I'm coming," Bart growled. He pulled the chaise lounge out of the way and opened the door. Tony burst through like a thunderstorm.

"I can't raise Mitchum on the radio. He should have been back by now. If he screws up his part . . ."

Bart interrupted him. "Jack would've known what to do. You should have thought before you . . ." He broke off abruptly. "Get out to the ship. There's a back-up number in the log book. Call it. Maybe Mitch got a late start or ran into bad weather. It's a long flight. I'm leaving for town to do my thing. Get back on ship and do yours."

Tony's reluctance to leave was evident, as well as his abhorrence at being bossed by anyone, especially someone younger. As he debated his course of action, Bart grabbed my arm and hustled me past this evil-looking, bad-tempered man. We raced down the stairs with Tony on our heels, cursing all the way. Bart grabbed my purse from the rolltop desk and thrust it at me as we ran to the car.

"Keys!"

I jumped in the passenger side of my car and Bart slid behind the wheel, reaching for the keys with one hand and hitting the door locks with the other.

Tony reached the car as the locks clicked and pounded on the roof. I was glad his words were lost in the roar of the engine.

"Okay, Sir Galahad. Where are we going now that you've rescued me from the fire-breathing dragon?" I asked.

"First stop is breakfast. Stern's Wharf or the Sea Cove? Or do you have another favorite I don't know about? We can go anywhere you like."

"You know I love the Sea Cove. I'd love the sun, sand, and seagulls even if their food wasn't wonderful. But it is!"

Santa Barbara, the nearest city, was our destination when we needed something from "town." I loved the old Spanish flavor of whitewashed adobe spilling to the bay, where rows of palm trees outlined the beach. I'd found in our travels this was one of the most beautiful cities on the coast—in fact, on any coast.

The drive to town was pleasant, winding down golden hills along a twisting road with frequent glimpses of the blue Pacific Ocean.

I thought I'd try again to get some answers. "Are you ready to answer a few questions?"

Bart glanced sideways at me and smiled. "You never have a few questions and I'm never ready for the barrage. How about if you answer a few instead?"

"Like?"

Bart nodded at my left hand. "Who's the lucky guy? I see someone's staked his claim. When are you getting married?"

I hated the tone in his voice and the insinuation that I was property to be staked out or claimed. I hated that he had left without a word, disappeared for five years, and now came back into my life as if nothing had happened.

"Milton J. Hollingsworth, III," I answered, hoping to freeze out further questions with the chill in my voice. "Your turn. Where are we going?"

"Santa Barbara. When are you getting married?"

"We haven't set a date."

"Why not? How long have you been engaged? What's wrong with him?"

"That's three questions. I've been busy. We've been engaged for over a year and there's nothing wrong with him. Why are we going to Santa Barbara? What plan am I part of? What about a photographer?"

"We have errands to run, and photographers take pictures. What does Milton do for a living? Why hasn't he swept you off your feet like any other red-blooded male would have? Or are you cohabiting and just haven't gotten around to a marriage license yet?" With the last question, he looked at me sharply.

I ignored his implications. "You didn't answer the question about the plan. Your exact words last night were: 'You know the plan. She's all mine and if you lay a finger on her, I'll kill you. Nothing works without her and she has to be in picture-perfect condition.' What plan?"

Bart laughed. "You still have a memory like a computer. The plan is very long and complicated, and we don't have time to do it justice. You didn't answer my last three questions."

"Those answers are very long and complicated, and we don't have time to do them justice either. Besides, I don't see that it's any of your business who I'm engaged to or what he's like."

"Sorry. Just a big brotherly interest. I want to make sure my little princess is going to be well taken care of, that's all."

Big brotherly interest! Was that it? Since he took that tack, I shifted gears abruptly.

"Bart, tell me about Dad," I asked softly. "Where has he been all these years? Why is he associated with these filthy kidnappers? How can we find him? He needs help." I ended on a pleading note. No loving brother could disregard an appeal for help.

Bart was quiet. I could tell he was formulating his answer carefully.

"I don't know how to find him. I agree he needs help. My hands are full right now."

"That's no answer at all! What are we going to do?"

"How about ordering breakfast?" His reply was low and resigned as he turned into the parking lot at Ledbetter Beach.

We ordered at the window of the Sea Cove and neither of us spoke as we took a table on the beach to watch the tide come in. I studied Bart who seemed miles away in thought. The college girls at the next table eyed him, too. I looked at him as they must have seen him. He was the ideal California beach boy: tall, slender, good-looking, with an athletic build, white blonde hair, a golden tan and startlingly blue eyes. Eyes that stared vacantly into space. He had a different look now that puzzled me. Different life-style? More worldly?

"Earth to Bart. Come in, please. What's the overpowering reason for this trip to town? I think I have a right to know."

Suddenly he turned his chair to face me and stared intently into my eyes. He reached across the table for my hand, as if he were gathering courage before speaking. Just then our breakfast came. Of course. We sat quietly while a courteous young man placed our plates on the table.

I waited for Bart to speak, but he stared into his plate, toying with his omelette.

"You were going to say . . ." I prompted, between bites of banana pecan waffles.

"Breakfast before business. Then we can walk around the bluffs and talk."

"In case you haven't noticed, the tide is coming in and the beach is gone."

"Sorry, Alli. I guess I have more pressing matters on my mind. How's your breakfast?"

"Fantastic, as always." I should probably have been too upset by all this to eat, but lack of food in the last couple of days had left me ravenous.

We finished breakfast in silence, then drove east to the Santa Barbara Marina and Stern's Wharf. Bart parked near Dolphin Fountain and we walked up the sidewalk paralleling the beach. I was careful to put space between us.

We dodged blade skaters, tourists in surrey-type pedal cars, joggers, and bicyclists. Finally he turned toward a rocky area on the beach. The incoming tide roared toward the rocks, crashing with a fanfare of spray. Bart found a dry rock and pulled me next to him.

When I looked into his face, I was shocked to see the anguish there. "Bart, are you ill?" The sound of the surf nearly drowned out his reply.

"No. I have something monumental to tell you and I don't know where to start, or how to tell you, or how much to tell you."

"Tell me how I'm involved and go from there."

Once again he reached for my hand, studying it as if the answer to his dilemma was there. I withdrew it. Brothers didn't hold hands with their little sisters.

"Allison, do you trust me? Will you trust me?"

I thought for a minute. "I used to. Not anymore."

"Why?"

"You need reasons?"

"Yes."

What can I tell him? That what I thought was a schoolgirl crush was much more? That I am a psychological mess since my father, then he, disappeared from my life? That I couldn't even marry the one steady guy who had patiently tried to help me work through my paranoia? I don't think so.

Instead I said, "Why would I trust a kidnapper of children?"

Silence.

Finally, he spoke. "I need you to trust me."

"I'm sorry, Bart. I've not seen anything that gives me reason to trust you. You won't answer my questions. You're holding two children hostage. You associate with evil and cruel men. Not much reason for trust, do you think?"

Bart stood up, took both of my hands in his and pulled me close, stifling my objections, speaking softly, pleading, almost in a whisper.

"Remember the pretend games we used to play idling away endless summer days? Allison, I need you to do something for me that I hope won't be too distasteful or inconvenient. Will you help me?"

"Do I get to know what it is before I answer?" I stepped away slightly, but he held my hands fast. My close proximity to him was unbearable.

"I need you to pretend that you love me, that you trust

me completely. I need you to go along with everything I say or do for the next few days and not ask any questions. I need your total commitment to me, to this."

I couldn't breathe. I tried to pull away, to turn from his probing, searching gaze. I wanted to run as fast and far as I could go before he realized what he was doing to me, but he wouldn't let go.

"The panic on your face speaks volumes. I realize you're engaged, but I promise to return you to your fiancé unscathed. Agreed?"

"This is the plan I'm part of?" I fought to control my voice, to sound normal.

"Yes. I'm sorry it worked out this way, but the whole thing pivots on you—and your performance."

"What kind of performance? Who's the audience? What are the consequences of wrong lines and missed cues?"

Bart pulled me closer, gently touching his finger to my lips to stop the questions. I twisted my head away. *Don't touch me,* I wanted to scream. *Don't do this to me!*

"You were a master of make believe. Help me weave a spell that Tony and everyone else will believe. Will it be so hard for you to pretend just for a few days that you love me?"

"Yes. That would be too hard." *Was he so dense he didn't realize what he asked?* "My pretending days are far behind me. I'm sorry, Bart. First of all, it wouldn't be fair to Milton. Please, let go."

"Would it convince you if you knew this was your father's plan, not mine?"

That forced me to meet his gaze. "Is that true?"

"Yes."

"Why would my father ask something like that of me?"

"For reasons you'll understand and agree with totally."

"After this is over."

Bart hesitated. "Unfortunately, yes."

"I have only your word. My father can't corroborate your story since he conveniently disappeared."

"Where did the cynicism come from, Allison? You used to be the most trusting, optimistic person I knew. What happened?"

I looked him straight in the eye. "You haven't a clue, have you?" He didn't. I could tell by the look on his face.

"If anything can save your father and get your family back together, it will be this one thing. That's probably more than I should have told you. Jack was to have broached this."

He'd strummed the one chord that would make me do it, the only motivation strong enough for me to allow myself to undergo the pain I knew this would bring.

His look was so intense I felt my face flush.

"Yes," I said finally.

"Remember the terms. No questions. You'll do exactly as I say until this is wrapped up. You'll pretend to be swept off your feet and go along with absolutely everything I propose. In short, you'll put yourself completely in my hands for the duration."

"Do I have your solemn promise it's my father's plan? His desire that I do this? That your only motivation is to help him?"

"My solemn oath."

"I'll do it. But I've some stipulations of my own. The pretext will end as soon as we're out of sight of anyone. You will not touch or kiss me unnecessarily, and Milton will have to know what I'm doing."

Bart's voice was cold and sarcastic. "Is that all?"

I opened my mouth to add a couple more I'd just thought of when he grabbed me by the arms and yanked me nearly nose to nose with him. His face was expressionless, but his voice was low and exasperated. "Listen carefully, you little fool. I'm not any happier about this crazy scheme than you are, but there are several lives that depend on it—yours and mine being the least of them. Do you understand this is the role of your life—literally? You have to live and breathe this pretense if it kills you—because if you don't, Tony will! Do you understand?"

"You're bruising my arms."

"I'm sorry." The look was softer, but the tone still intense, his fingers still dug into my arms. "Will you do it? On my terms?"

"I'll do it. If you'll let go."

"Your role starts now. If you throw yourself into it and pick up your cues as well as you used to, we'll pull it off. Ready?"

I took a deep breath and nodded. But I wasn't ready for what happened next.

Bart pulled me into his arms and kissed me. A glow started as his lips touched mine and spread like fire all through me. I was so surprised, I couldn't protest. So shocked, I didn't try to pull away. So stunned, I let him—even let myself enjoy this frightening but exhilarating sensation I'd never felt before with anyone else. An ache started deep within me and I melted against him, returning his kiss with a passion that suddenly shocked me to my senses.

I pulled away, trembling, frightened at losing control. I didn't like not being in control. I turned my back to Bart so he couldn't see what he'd done to me.

His arms encircled me from behind and he put his lips close to my ear. "I always wondered what it would be like to kiss you, Princess. It was worth the wait."

I stiffened.

He got the message. His tone was all business, though he didn't release me.

"The only place we'll be able to talk freely is where there's a lot of background noise. Today's technology has obliterated privacy. Even whispers can be picked up by parabolic mikes. We have to assume that every room and every car will be bugged. From this minute, you're on stage, so play your role to the hilt. Smile and pretend this is the happiest day of your life. I'll do my best to make it that."

He turned me around and looked down at me. *Checking my reaction? Compose yourself, Allison. Take control of the situation.* I reached up and touched his cheek.

"You certainly know all the right moves. I shouldn't have any trouble following your cues at all. Shall we get this show on the road? No pun intended."

Bending down, he gently kissed the tip of my nose and ever so softly brushed a kiss on my lips.

"Let's get to it!" he said as he dragged me to the car.

"Do I get to know where we're going?"

"I think there was some mention of no questions." He gave me a stern look and pantomimed a listening device. "Here's a challenge for you. Today, see if you can get by without asking a single question. Personally, I don't think you can last fifteen minutes without asking questions."

"I'll accept that challenge. You'll be amazed at the self-discipline I've acquired these last few years while you've been off improving the world. I assume that's what you've been doing . . . that wasn't a question."

Bart laughed, a genuine sound that came from deep within, a sound I'd always loved.

"First stop, my apartment. I don't want to embarrass you by appearing in public looking like this, especially when you look like you just stepped out of a fashion magazine."

I blushed at his compliment. "Thank you, kind sir. I didn't know you had an apartment in town."

"Princess, there's a lot you don't know about me." I sensed a shift in mood, then as though he was determined to keep things light, he smiled. "I've had this apartment since you were about fourteen. After high school graduation, I wanted to be on my own. I found a nice old couple who couldn't do their yard work anymore. In exchange for that and keeping their old car running, they gave me an apartment over their garage while I finished college. When I left the area, I kept the apartment so I'd have a mailing address. I didn't want my folks' address to show up on my mail in case . . ." He stopped.

"In case someone was looking for you. That was a statement. If I'm wrong, correct me."

"Very observant—and clever. I almost mistook it for a question. Yes. I didn't want to lead anyone to the folks. Come on up. I'll only be a minute."

His apartment was cozy and neat, a sitting/bedroom with a day bed, two chairs and a coffee table, a kitchenette with a table for two and a bathroom and closet. I relaxed in a brown tweed overstuffed chair and bathed in the radiance of the morning sun.

Can I handle this? What would "this" consist of? I always said I'd do anything to have my father back, no matter what the cost. This was certainly the ultimate price.

In what seemed only a minute, Bart emerged from the bathroom in tan linen slacks and a white shirt open at the collar, holding a blue silk tie the color of his eyes.

"Hope you don't mind if I carry this and don it at the appropriate time. I'm a real believer in the 'California Casual' approach to dressing. Ready?"

"Lead on, Lochinvar. I'm ready for whatever this beautiful

day will bring."

Bart tilted my chin up and looked so deeply into my eyes he seemed to be searching the depths of my soul.

"I hope you are, Princess, with all my heart."

Chapter Six

Opening the car door, he smiled and bowed gallantly. “Your chariot awaits.”

“Before I enter, slave, I command you to tell me where we’re going.”

“To the artisan, to pick up something I left there, M’Lady.”

In a matter of minutes we arrived at our destination. A jewelry store? Bart opened my door and met my questioning glance with a bemused smile, but not one word of explanation.

“Good morning, Mr. Welch. Is it ready for the lady?” Bart asked the small round man who greeted us as we entered.

“All ready, sir.” He peered intently at me over his half glasses. “My goodness, you were right. It is the same color as her eyes. Amazing. A wonderful choice. And a remarkable gem. Very rare.”

“Thank you very much, Mr. Welch,” Bart said. “I appreciate your rushing this for me.” He paid Mr. Welch, took the white velvet case from him, then grasped me firmly by the elbow and ushered me out the door. “I know you’re bursting with questions. Soon you’ll know what it’s all about.”

He was playing this to the hilt and enjoying every minute of it. Was it all make believe, or was he simply falling back on our old camaraderie of years ago? I sat patiently while we drove down Anacapa Street, turning into the parking garage across from the courthouse.

"You have business at the courthouse," I stated, making it sound more like a statement than the question it was as we jaywalked across the busy street, dodging cars.

"The most important business of my life," he said mischievously. He held my hand tightly as we walked past the Spirit of the Ocean fountain and into the cool semi-darkness of the courthouse.

I felt transported to Andalusian Spain each time I entered here. Brilliantly colored Tunisian tiles lined stairways and walls, Islamic and Byzantine archways led to the loggias, and heavy wooden Spanish doors added to the old world atmosphere.

Bart led me up the blue and gold tiled stairway in the tower well with its Mudejar ceiling and murals painted high on the walls. We waited for the elevator on the second floor where the stained glass Rose Window added a Romanesque flavor to the foyer. So many cultures were so wonderfully mixed in this romantic old building.

No one seemed to be paying attention to us, and neither of us spoke as the elevator droned to the fourth floor. This was ridiculous. Two grown-ups acting out a play with no audience. A play I wanted no part in.

We climbed the steep flight of stairs to the tower and were met by Santa Barbara's famous fresh sea breeze and bright warm sun.

The beauty of the scene spreading eighty-five feet below us was spectacular. The ocean was a deep blue, the clouds were dazzling white, and the mountains were shades of green dappled by white houses with orange-tiled roofs. We leaned against the wrought-iron railing, drinking in the sights, sounds, and smells spread before us like a feast.

"Allison . . ." Bart took a deep breath. He drew me down to the cold concrete bench and took my hands in his, facing me, but avoiding my gaze. I waited. Did he need to carry the act this far?

"Allison, I don't know how else to say this. I love you. Will you marry me?"

I nearly fell off the bench.

"I think you love me, at least, you did. I've changed and you don't know anything about me since I left Margo's. You'll have to trust me—to rely on what you remember about me and how I was . . ."

"Bart, I can't marry you. I'm engaged to be married." *This can't be happening. It's not real. What's he doing?*

"You'll have to tell him the engagement is off. Tell him it was me you always loved. Tell him you've postponed the wedding hoping I'd come back, and now I have. Just tell me you'll marry me."

I pulled away and moved to the railing, gripping it until my knuckles were white. *He had it right. Every single reason he'd just recited was precisely on the money. How did he know?* That old familiar anguish hit the pit of my stomach. I wouldn't let it incapacitate me again. *Get command of the situation, Allison.*

I turned to face him and caught a glimpse of movement behind a pillar. Was there really someone here? Were we actually playing to an audience? Who knew we'd be here? *Okay. I can do this.*

"It's not fair to do that to Milton." I thought of my fiance. *I'd told him about Bart from the beginning to discourage him. He knew I didn't love him, but he was confident I eventually would. "After all," he'd said, "who couldn't love 100 million dollars of one of America's oldest monied families?"*

On cue, Bart moved to the railing to take me in his arms.

"This is too corny," I whispered, barely able to breathe because of his closeness.

He had me trapped against the railing. My stomach tightened, throat constricted, vision blurred, and a pounding began in the back of my head. It was happening again.

"Bart, let me go. I can't." That was as much as I got out before his mouth smothered the rest of my cry. I wanted him to hold me, wanted to return his kiss. But I couldn't put myself through the physical and psychological pain I'd suffered for the last five years. *No! Don't do this to me! I'm not as strong as I thought. I can't go through with your plan.*

Tears streamed down my face, salting my lips. I couldn't stop crying. *Where's your self-control? That self-discipline you're so proud of? Get hold of yourself.*

With all the energy I could muster, I pushed him away. "You weren't listening," I sobbed.

"I heard you." He wiped my tears with the back of his hand. "But you can and you will, because I love you—and I know you love me. Take off that ridiculous diamond." He pulled my engagement ring from my finger and dropped it in my right hand.

From the white velvet box, Bart produced the most exquisite emerald I'd ever seen and slid it onto my finger, kissing my fingertips gently.

"My little princess. I love you so much! I wish I could build you a beautiful castle and protect you from all the bad in the world. But life isn't the fairy tale we used to pretend it was. Today's dragons are greedy, evil men who stop at nothing to get what they want. With this ring, I promise you love and protection as long as there is life in this body. But I have something more precious than this ring—or my love—to give you . . . something more precious than life itself. I've found—"

He was interrupted by a noise on the other side of the tower, and a frisson of fear shivered through me. Then I heard footsteps descending the metal stairs. Someone else had been up here with us and had heard everything we said! How had they known we'd be here?

Bart put his arm around my shoulder, pulled me next to him, and kissed my forehead. "You're terrific," he whispered. "The tears were a perfect touch. Keep up the good work. Our audience is in place."

If he only knew. This was the hardest thing I'd ever done. What was the reason for it? How could this pretense possibly help Dad? What had he meant—something more precious than the expensive emerald, or his love, or life itself? Once, nothing would have been more precious to me than his love.

Suddenly Bart glanced at his watch. "We'd better get in gear!"

He sped up as we left the courthouse, swooping me along with one arm around my waist, chatting about something I wasn't digesting. My mind was awhirl with questions.

"I assume I'm allowed to ask questions now."

"Not yet. This short amount of time would hardly be a challenge for you."

We turned into a long, low, vine-covered building that proclaimed Dr. Steven Jones on the door.

"A doctor's office?"

"To get married, we've got to have a blood test."

"Wait a minute!" I stopped abruptly.

Bart's blue eyes twinkled like Christmas tree lights. I hadn't seen him so animated since his father had given him flying lessons for Christmas one year.

"This is no time to get cold feet, Allison." Bart grabbed my elbow and pinched a pressure point. In my ear, he hissed, "You promised to do exactly as I said."

I smiled sweetly, pretending to kiss his cheek, and whispered in his ear, "The agreement didn't mention marriage!"

The nurse interrupted our exchange to usher us into a small office where a technician waited, though several other people were in the waiting room. It was as if we were expected—but they couldn't have known . . . could they?

The next few hours were a blur of stops. First the Hall of Records on the corner of Anapamu and Anacapa Streets. Huge, heavy wrought-iron-covered glass doors were the first things to slow Bart down all morning.

He pulled a pen from his pocket, $56 from his wallet, and announced to the clerk we wanted a marriage license. This would be interesting. How far would Bart carry the farce? Surely we weren't going to go through with it?

"Bart, I don't have a wedding dress, there are invitations to have printed . . . nothing is ready for a wedding. Mom's in Athens. I can't get married without her." Suddenly I remembered Dad's warning. Mom was in danger. She was supposed to be hiding.

Bart glanced up from the papers he was filling out. "Your mom should be on her way here right now."

"She's giving lectures all week in Athens and won't be back for ten days."

"A messenger was sent yesterday to bring her. I've taken care of the dress and the flowers and the invitations."

"I don't even get to pick my own wedding dress?" This was getting scary.

"Remember the day I caught you sketching your wedding dress? You were still in braces and pigtails. I retrieved that sketch from the wastebasket and I've had it ever since. I had the dress made in Hong Kong."

"I'm flabbergasted! I don't know what to say!"

"That's a first. You're never at a loss for words." He became serious. "I've always loved you, Princess. Even when you were a skinny little pest that followed me everywhere, I knew you'd grow up to be extraordinary and I wanted you to be all mine."

"You're laying it on awfully thick," I whispered in his ear, pretending to kiss him. *Why does he say the very thing I've wanted to hear all these years?*

As we left the Hall of Records, I was close to tears. The memory of the wedding I'd planned so long ago came flooding back. Dad would come from wherever he'd been to give me away, then never leave again.

Bart paused under the shady branches of an ancient tree. "I want this to be perfect for you, Princess. I remember the rest of your dream. We'll see about making it all come true."

Tears spilled from my eyes. I dropped my head so Bart couldn't see, but he tilted my chin up and wiped them away. I tried to pull away from his touch.

"Trust me," he whispered. "I'll do everything within my power to make you happy for the rest of your life and beyond. Do you believe I can do that? Allison, I've found the most wonderful thing in the world. I can't wait to share it with you, when we can talk without being overheard. It's too precious for the wrong ears." His voice was urgent, intense. "Maybe I've moved too fast. Should we stop at La Arcada for a cold drink?"

"No, Sir Galahad! Forward with your plans to rescue this poor damsel from her distress!"

Bart gazed at me for a long minute, then his blue eyes sparkled.

"The next stop: someone to perform the ceremony!"

"You've neglected to inform the bride of her wedding date."

"Didn't I tell you? Sunday." Having dropped that bombshell, Bart slammed the car door before I could say a word. When he got in the other side, he reached across and shushed my question with a fingertip. I felt like biting it.

At the corner of Los Olivos and Santa Barbara Street, Bart pulled to the curb in front of a large, white church.

"What church is this?"

"A very special one," Bart said as he put on his blue silk tie. "You've heard of the Mormons? We'll meet with the bishop." He turned to me. "He's not just a priest. He's . . ." Bart stopped as he glanced in the rear view mirror and opened his door. "I'll tell you later." He was clearly troubled.

So was I. As we approached the door, I pulled him into the shadow of a large tree.

"Hold me for just a minute before we go in."

Bart stopped in surprise. I put my arms around his neck and whispered in his ear, "But not too close. What do you think you're doing? We can't go before a bishop and ask him to pretend to marry us!"

"Play along, Princess. Your dad planned it perfectly." His arms felt so natural around my waist.

"Bart, I can't lie to a priest! And stop holding me so close!" His answer was to press me closer and kiss my neck before he let me go. I pushed him away and turned to look up and down the street. This charade was ridiculous! No one was watching.

Bart must have read my thoughts. He pulled me inside the church, and whispered in my ear, "Look for the white Mercedes when we leave."

I went along reluctantly, though I didn't have much choice. He had a grip on my arm that death itself couldn't have freed.

Beautiful pictures depicting the life of Christ adorned the walls of the long hallway leading to the small, neat office of a physically fit, fairly young man in shirt and tie, sans clerical robes.

"Good morning, Bishop O'Hare." Bart's greeting was warm and familiar. He knew this man!

"Good morning, Bart. Allison, I'm glad to finally meet you." Bishop O'Hare's handshake was firm, his eyes friendly, but penetrating. I felt he could discern my very thoughts. *Finally meet me? How long had Bart known him? What had he told him?*

I tried to sit calmly and look like a bride-to-be but I was screaming inside. *I can't do this! I can't lie to this man of God. What will happen to me if I do? Then again, what will happen if I don't?*

The interview that followed was interesting, to say the least, and I found myself liking this personable young Bishop O'Hare with the wild red tie.

I was so busy formulating some story of my own without actually lying that I hardly heard Bart's replies to the bishop's questions. He asked me only background questions which I could answer truthfully. I'd known Bart all my life. He'd always been my best friend and we'd shared a very special relationship. No, we'd never had any trouble communicating. He'd always been kind and considerate and protective of me in every way. Bart fairly beamed at my answers. I left out the part about the last five years.

After a few minutes of pre-marital counseling, Bishop O'Hare uttered the words that made carrying this deceit any further seem positively sinful, no matter how important the outcome might appear.

"I'm sure you both agree that entering into marriage

covenants is never anything to be taken lightly. Marriage is a covenant between God and the two of you, an eternal commitment."

"Yes, sir," Bart said, looking straight at me, holding my hand so tight I couldn't withdraw it. "We've always felt the same way. And we'll make it eternal as soon as possible."

What did he mean? Bart's unusual phrasing caught my attention, as well as the light in his eyes, his excited expression.

We had talked a great deal about forever, especially the last time I'd seen Bart, when I thought he'd proposed to me—just before he'd disappeared from my life! Was Bart really serious about going through with this? He couldn't be! What would he do when it was all over? Get an annulment? That was a pretty short forever.

I was having trouble breathing. I'd never fainted in my life, but I was about to. I'd never stifled a scream so long, either. *I must get out of here!*

Bishop O'Hare agreed to come to "Margo's Mansion," as everyone called it, to marry us on Sunday at 5:00 p.m. He said something about seeing Bart "shortly thereafter in the waters of baptism," but I wasn't listening anymore. I couldn't leave fast enough.

As we stepped from the church, I looked for a white Mercedes. A bright shiny new one, with chrome gleaming in the sun, was parked on Los Olivos.

Chapter Seven

The sight of the Mercedes stifled the questions I was prepared to fire at first opportunity. I had to find another way to talk to Bart. Having him hold me was too disconcerting, like ordering a beating for myself.

Next stop was the white stucco building housing the Santa Barbara *Statesman-Press.* Unfolding a piece of paper he had tucked in his back pocket, he walked up to the counter and handed it to the receptionist at the desk.

"Will you please see that the society editor gets this?" he asked, a smile crinkling his eyes.

She scanned the paper, then looked up in surprise, first at Bart, then me. Her mouth dropped open. Bart guided me to the door, chuckling out loud. Over my shoulder, I saw her run toward the back of the office, waving the paper.

"What was that all about?" Again, my curiosity won over my self-control.

"More questions? I thought it was time we threw a little spice into the life of Santa Barbara society."

Back to State Street and Paseo Nuevo. Our first stop was a flower and candle shop where Bart laid another piece of paper on the counter. "Will you fill this order for me?"

The tall, elegant lady looked it over and observed coolly, "These are very rare, sir, and very expensive."

"If you're at the Flower Mart in Los Angeles at 2:00 a.m. when the grower delivers them, you can get everything on that list. I know how much they cost and how many are delivered each day. Will you please deliver the entire order on Sunday?"

"I'm sorry, sir. We don't deliver on Sunday," she sniffed.

"Please deliver that order, as described, to the address on that paper."

She glanced at the address, then looked up in awe, her cool elegance only slightly compromised.

"Yes, sir. I'll personally deliver them. What time would you like them to arrive?"

"No later than 3:00 p.m. Also, we'll need candles to match, about four dozen, I'd say." Margo's name worked magic.

We ducked down a picturesque alley filled with shops, stopping at one hidden away at the very end. It was a boutique crammed with marvelous creations, but the masterpiece adorned a mannequin in the center of the miniature shop. It was the most exquisite wedding dress I'd imagined in my life!

Lace in a Lilliputian flower design covered the bodice. Over each petal was sewn a teardrop-shaped pearl, and over each leaf was . . . an emerald! The white satin skirt was slim and straight, with an extravagant train attached at the waist that fanned out like a peacock's tail. Delicate lace edged the shallow scooped neckline with gleaming freshwater pearls playing peek-a-boo in the ruffle.

I stopped inside the doorway and stared. Bart edged around to see my face.

"I'm pleased you like it."

"This is mine?"

"It's your design. Of course, I made a few additions. I hope the pearls and emeralds are acceptable."

"It's been so long since I even thought about it!" *How do I stop this? I feel like I'm being carried downstream faster and faster toward a waterfall, and there's no way out.* I turned to Bart, nearly ill with panic. Couldn't he see?

"Here's your tiara. A crown fit for a royal princess." From a box on a chair behind the dress, he produced an emerald and pearl creation that could easily belong to a queen. He placed it on my head with a flourish, then backed away and cocked his head to one side.

"Something isn't quite right." He tilted the tiara at a dangerous angle on the back of my head and kissed the tip of my nose, cocked his head again and looked at me.

"Still not quite right." Removing the tiara, he gathered me in his arms and kissed me. It happened again. The tingle . . . then the fire. I tried to break away.

"I love you so much, Allison," Bart said softly. "I want your life to be one happy surprise after another—forever."

I couldn't stand it another minute! I turned to run out the door—to get away from him, away from this charade, but he had a firm grip on me.

"I'm sorry," he whispered, his voice cold and hurt. "I didn't realize that would have such an adverse effect. Do you hate me so much you can't stand to hear me say that?"

Bart thrust the tiara into my hands and spun out the door. Madame Shuang remained discreetly in the back of her shop till Bart left, then appeared with a timid smile and a slight bow. I took a deep breath to compose myself.

"Does it please you?" she asked softly. She was lovely, with shining black hair wound atop her head like a crown of lustrous ebony. She seemed out of place here with the air of elegance and refinement she couldn't hide in spite of her lowered eyes, timorous smile, and subservient bow. I could easily picture her in an embassy or a palace, but not a tiny shop in a picturesque alleyway in Santa Barbara.

"It's breathtakingly beautiful."

"My son made it for Mr. Allan in Hong Kong."

"Your son is an artist."

She showed me into a closet-sized dressing room, and while I slipped into the dress, she disappeared into the recesses of her shop, reappearing with an armful of gossamer sheer tulle. The dress was a perfect fit.

"My son did a fine job on this dress, but you make it even more beautiful." She placed the emerald and pearl tiara atop my black curls and gathered the tulle in her arms, tucking here, gathering there, pinning and pulling, then stepped back.

I turned slowly and for the first time saw in the mirror detailed cutwork on the train with pearls and emeralds cascading to the floor and for yards after. I felt like a fairy princess.

Someone entered the shop and Madame Shuang excused herself, but she was back immediately.

"It is the photographer for you, Miss Alexander. I will carry the train so you can be photographed by the fountain."

Through the dressing room door I saw a sharply dressed young woman with straight long blonde hair that fell across her face when she moved.

Accompanying her was a huge bear of a man sporting a shaggy beard. Camera equipment bulged from every pocket in his baggy tweed jacket and he looked as crumpled as she did chic. The blonde woman spoke first.

"Miss Alexander, I'm Cory Black from the Statesman-Press. Congratulations! I must say, I have never seen anything so beautiful as your dress! I understand it was handmade for you in Hong Kong."

As she spoke, I let myself be swept along by this current, helpless to stop it.

"Is Margo's money financing this wedding? Just what is your connection with her, other than your having lived on her estate? I understand she may actually be present at the ceremony." She watched my expression closely as she bombarded me with questions.

Hoping my surprise didn't show at that last tidbit, I dropped my head so my veil fell forward, pretending to trip on the step from one level to another.

"That would set things stirring around here, wouldn't it?" I smiled brightly. *What did Margo have to do with my wedding? Where would Cory Black get an idea like that?*

"Where's Margo been all these years and what's she been doing? Why is she returning for your wedding?"

I tried to smile sweetly through the flash and the questions, but my smile was wearing thin when Bart appeared from the White House Men's Store down the promenade, resplendent in silver tux and top hat with emerald green cummerbund and tie.

He came straight to me, his eyes never leaving mine all the way across the patio. I started trembling all over. What now? He reached for my hands, seemingly oblivious to the small crowd watching the photo session.

"I'm sorry, Allison. I couldn't help myself. I was trying on my tux and saw you through the window. I've never seen such a breathtaking vision of loveliness in my life." He had a dazzling smile on his face, but his eyes weren't smiling anymore. At least now I knew he was acting. Before I wasn't sure.

"You shouldn't see me in my dress before the wedding!"

The Bear snapped a picture of us before I fled back to the privacy of Madame Shuang's boutique, with Madame struggling to keep the train from the sidewalk. As I rounded the corner I heard Cory Black firing questions at Bart about Margo.

What had Margo to do with this and why did her name come up now? The story was always revived around the anniversary of her disappearance, with the same questions repeated each time. But why now, why in connection with the wedding?

I changed quickly and escaped out the back door, but Bart caught me and guided me firmly back to the car. The air bristled with tension.

Bart chose his words carefully. "I know I've swept you off your feet and you're still in a state of shock with the whirlwind of preparations. I'm sure you're worried about how to tell Milton you're getting married, but not to him. Are you up to continuing today, or do you need to rest?"

Was he asking me if I wanted to back out? *Yes, I want out,* I wanted to scream. *I need to get away from here.* I needed the exertion of a good run right now to clear my head, to get away from the emotional exhaustion of being so close to Bart in this ridiculous situation.

"There were a couple of errands we needed to run before we go back to the house. A few groceries . . ." He left the rest of his statement hanging in the air, but I got the message. If I quit, what about Sunny and Boomer? Then I thought of Dad. They were all in far worse trouble than I was. All I had to suffer was Bart's arms around me and his kisses. The very things I'd dreamed about for years. Surely I could endure that for Dad.

"On to the errands!" I tried to sound jaunty. I had the prickly feeling we were being watched.

While Bart got groceries, I picked out a stuffed dolphin and a couple of books and games for Sunny and Boomer to keep them entertained in their tree house prison.

On the way home, Bart kept glancing in his rearview mirror. I turned around. The white Mercedes was following us.

Bart took off his watch and, pressing one of the many buttons on the side, exposed a new face. He swept his side of the car with it, then handed it to me. As I waved it in front of the visor's vanity mirror, the dial went crazy, like a miniature geiger counter. A bug. Our conversations were being monitored.

"When we get back, will you take me down to the beach?"

"Great idea." He knew what I needed—a place to talk. I wasn't sure which was worse, having Bart hold me and kiss me as if he meant it, knowing it was a pretense, or having him cold and quiet, thinking I hated him when exactly the opposite was true. Why was this ridiculous charade necessary? How would the deception help Dad? Who was in that white Mercedes?

Chapter Eight

As the car stopped in the driveway, I jumped out and ran for the cottage.

"Allison, wait." It was a command. Bart's tone implied I'd better listen.

I waited on the step. He came close behind me, without touching me, and hissed, "Don't leave my side while we're on the estate. I trust I won't have to repeat that."

"I was going to change clothes so you could take me to the beach, remember?"

"Yes." His voice was cold and hard.

The cottage was open. Someone had been smoking here. No wonder Bart didn't want me going anywhere alone.

"Tony could have been waiting for you. Don't run off alone."

"Message received," I whispered, eating humble pie. After a quick change of clothes, we walked to the beach in silence, holding hands for the benefit of anyone watching, a concession I felt necessary until we could communicate.

We sat close together on the rocks where we could talk, but couldn't be heard over the roar of the surf, even with the best mike. Bart was careful not to touch me.

"You misread my reaction," I explained. "I don't hate you. I never could."

"Then what was that look on your face? I'm not asking anything so hard, am I?"

If only you knew.

"You didn't tell me we were supposed to get married in this little subterfuge. How will Milton feel, discovering we're married and not hearing a single word from me? You said you didn't like this deceit any better than I did, but you're so good at it, you make it believable. Bart, I need some answers. You speak of trust—can't you trust me enough to tell me what it's all about? I can't imagine how our pretending to get married will help Dad and Sunny and Boomer—or us. Since it doesn't make sense, it seems so unproductive. Granted, I felt we were being watched all day, but by whom? And why? And who bugged the car? I need to know more."

"Your dad would have explained it better, but I didn't know how much I dared tell you. I thought you'd throw yourself into this role and have fun with it like we used to. I didn't realize how much you'd changed."

"Meaning?"

"For one thing, you're all grown up. I remembered you more as an adoring little sister. Well, not exactly a little sister, but . . ."

"I get the picture. Tell me why it's necessary." I didn't need to hear the "little sister" stuff again.

"Your father's with Interpol. The notification of his death in that explosion was fabrication. He was with the Office of Special Investigation in Vietnam, and the OSI used it as an excuse to let him disappear, gave him the identity of the dead terrorist, and had him infiltrate the group that tried to kill him. He "dismantled" the organization. By that time the war was over and he was ready to be resurrected, to resume his life with your family, when another blood bath occurred. Interpol needed his unique talents to ferret out the terrorists. In a nutshell, it turned into a career."

My instincts had been right. I knew my father wasn't like those loathsome creatures.

"Where do you come in?"

"Later. Company's coming." Bart nodded his head slightly at a small boat heading our way from the big ship. "Listen. I'll protect you with my life, but around Tony and Sam, adore me. Do whatever I tell you and stick to me. They have to believe you'll do anything for me—that you're so much in love you'd jump off a cliff if I asked. While we can talk safely—we have to find your dad. You sensed a place that was cold and damp. Other than the caves, where else fits that description?"

"Only behind the waterfall, but I'm sure he's not there. From the General, we'd have seen him come down the hill. I just remembered something else. Was he shot in the ballroom?"

"No. Why?"

"Did you look in the ballroom?"

Bart shook his head. "Not really. Just a glance."

"When I heard and sensed the shot, I could see a gold bass clef with blood running into it. That had to be the ballroom. Then I felt a sensation of falling. We need to start there. Do you know about the secret passageways in the house?"

"There's more than the one we used, but I don't know where. Do you still need that run on the beach or can we go take care of the things in the car before this boat full of trouble lands?"

The small boat from the ship would beach shortly. I had sufficient answers for now. I could continue the sham.

As we approached the driveway, Tony arrived—from town and spying on us, I'd guess. The white Mercedes was just leaving the estate. Tony barreled toward us, but Bart fired the first salvo.

"Where've you been, Tony? You're supposed to be on the ship. Did you talk to Mitchum?"

"Yes. He can't find her anywhere. She's disappeared."

Bart glanced at me, then led Tony a few feet away. Bart's voice was low. I couldn't decipher the words. Tony's raspy voice was louder.

"We need her. She's got to be here!"

Bart's reply was too low for me to understand. When he finished, Tony snarled, "If this doesn't work, you know what'll happen!"

Then Bart raised his voice. "Call him again. Have him ask the maid where she usually goes, a number where she can be reached. A little persuasion should convince the maid to cooperate. He's not to hurt her—just scare her. He'd better get on the ball. It's a fourteen-hour flight from Greece. And get that motley crew of yours back on ship. We don't need anyone finding that garbage cluttering up the estate."

Still cursing and threatening Bart, Tony rumbled down the lawn toward the beach. I assaulted Bart as he returned to get the groceries from the car.

"What are you going to do with my mother?"

"Bring her here for the wedding. . . ."

I launched myself at him, threw my arms around his neck, and pulled myself up to whisper in his ear. Bart's arms went around me, pressing me close, lifting me to hear.

"I received a message to warn Mom she's in danger," I whispered. "I left the message with Maria. If he can't find her, it's because Mom's hiding. Dad was afraid for her. Why would he tell her to hide if she needed to be brought here?"

"When was that?"

"The day after Dad was shot."

"After? Mmmm. That means he changed the plan. Maybe it's too dangerous to bring her here. We've got to find your dad and find out why he changed everything. Let's go to the ballroom. You know, you fit real nice here."

My face flushed. I let go.

"It's all right. I don't mind, if you don't," he laughed.

"We've got to find another way to communicate!" I hissed.

We headed for the cottage where we dumped the groceries on the kitchen table and grabbed a flashlight from one of the drawers. As we started up the lawn, we watched Tony and crew depart for the ship. The door to the mansion was unlocked. Apparently they were coming and going as if they lived here.

We started searching on opposite sides of the ballroom, dropping to the floor for a closer examination of each inlaid bass clef.

Then I found it. Though a clean-up had been attempted, a dark brown stain I could flake off remained in the crevices.

"Bart!"

The fireplace was within six feet. Approaching the filigree peacock, I remembered the last time I'd been in here. Someone *had* been watching me. This time I ran my hands over the peacock as I'd started to before, twisting and turning the emerald eyes, first one, then the other. Remembering the electronically controlled panels in the house, I pushed both emeralds at the same time. Whatever I expected to happen, didn't.

Bart was at my shoulder. "You think there's a secret passage here?"

"Yes, and I'm sure the emerald eyes activate the panel," I

whispered. I pushed one up and one down simultaneously. Voilá! The movement of something behind the gold peacock would probably have been imperceptible had I not been listening so intently.

We slipped behind the peacock into the fireplace. Bart turned on the flashlight, exposing an elevator in the right wall.

"Whoever designed these electronics was a genius. The panels are so silent you can't hear them operate. That feature, and Dad's warning, saved me from Tony."

"How did he warn you?"

How could I explain it without sounding ludicrous and melodramatic?

"I'm not sure exactly, but I get impressions, visual pictures, images. I know they're from Dad. Don't ask me how. I just know. The same way I've always known he was still alive, I guess."

Standing close to Bart in the tiny elevator after he pushed the down button, I experienced the same sensation of falling I felt when Dad was shot.

Bart switched off his light as the elevator stopped. The door slid silently open on total darkness, but the air was cool, wet, and the smell of the sea was heavy. The only sounds were waves lapping at rocks nearby.

"We're at sea level! No wonder I felt we were falling. We descended in seconds!" I whispered.

When we heard no sound but the sea, Bart flashed on the light and played it around the walls of the cave. There was no sign of Dad or anyone else.

The further into the tunnel we went, the closer we came to the sea. I was puzzled. When I visited the Blue Grotto on the Isle of Capri, light shimmered through the water, illuminating the cave, though little sunlight pierced the tiny entrance. An underwater entry allowed reflected light, but this was total darkness where no outside light penetrated.

I concentrated on trying to make contact. *Dad, Bart's with me. We want to help you. Tell me where you are.* Why had I mentioned Bart? Was there a possibility if I brought Bart to Dad he'd do something other than help? I pushed this thought from my mind and concentrated again. *Dad, can you hear me?*

Kindinos. Danger.

Dad, it's Allison. We're in the caves under the ballroom. Guide us to you.

"I hear him. He sounds weak and delirious."

Bart played his flashlight on the walls and ceiling of the passage that tunneled through solid rock, searching for another passage or a hidden door. "Allison, stop."

A weak voice directly below us drifted up. "Down here."

Bart shined the light on the floor of the cave. Inches from where we were standing, the rock floor disappeared into a black void. One more step and we'd have plunged over the edge onto the rocks below. Bart knelt, shining the light down. The water reflected our spot of light back at us, revealing a body.

"Steps against the wall." His voice was barely audible. Bart played the light down the long set of steps carved into the rock so I could see my way to the man lying half in the water. We moved Dad onto the tiny shelf of sand away from the lapping waves. Though he shivered with cold, his skin was hot.

Touching something wet, cold, and strange, I jumped back.

"Seaweed." Dad made a vain attempt to laugh as he reached weakly for my hand. "Stuffed in bullet hole."

His voice trailed off, weak from the exertion of speaking.

Was he still conscious?

Bart gently carried Dad up the stairs while I shined the light for them. "Over there," Dad pointed. His voice, muffled against Bart's shirt, was full of pain. Dad touched an indentation, like a deep chisel chip, and the wall opened.

It was unbelievable. There were so many computers, radios, and machines, that it could easily have been the communication center of a modern industry or airport. The air was warm and dry, like any modern office building with central air and fluorescent lights.

We eased Dad into the chair beside a bed in a small chamber.

"Let's get his wet clothes off before we put him on that clean bed," I said, attempting to strip the soaked, smelly shirt from his shoulders. His head fell back and I saw his face for the first time. I held his head where the light from the radio room illuminated his features. This was the first time I had actually seen my father in nearly twenty years.

Tears stung my eyes as I realized I could have passed him on the street and not recognized him.

Bart, sensitive to what I was feeling, gently pulled Dad's shirt off and unbuckled his belt.

"See if you can find some towels and water. There must be a bathroom somewhere," he said. I hurried to find something to wash away the salt, sand, and blood.

I found towels, antibiotics, and bandages, and set about dressing my father's injuries. I assumed the wound in his back indicated the bullet had gone all the way through. I poured antiseptic liberally over the front of his chest and bandaged it, then Bart helped me do the back.

As we settled him back on the bed, Dad opened his eyes.

"Can you handle seeing this old man face to face?" he mumbled, reaching for my face, but his hand dropped weakly. I picked it up and held it to my cheek.

"I've wanted to do this for so long." He paused, breathless at the great effort it took to speak. His hand dropped and his eyes closed.

"Dad!" Grabbing his shoulders, I started to shake him, fearing the worst.

"Careful . . . ," he grimaced, taking my hand from his wounded shoulder. "I'm not ready to die yet." Then he slipped back into unconsciousness.

I choked back the rising panic. I could not lose my father now! *Please let him live! I prayed. I need him. And I need so many answers only he can give me!* While I watched my father, Bart examined the radio room. "I knew there was a control center on the west coast," he said, "but here?"

Suddenly the radio crackled. The unmistakable sound of Gravel Voice shattered the quiet of the room. I shivered at the things I heard.

"Mitch, I don't care if you hafta search every one of those 1400 islands! Find that woman and get'er back here! She better be here by five o'clock Sunday or don't you come back."

"But, Tony . . ."

"Do whatever it takes, Mitch! I got Bart to worry about. I don't trust him or that broad. She's the key to this and he can't foul things up with her. So you get her mother back here pronto, do you hear me?"

The transmission ceased and the room was quiet.

Dad mumbled that he was cold, bitter cold. I tucked the blanket around his shoulders and wiped the perspiration from his face.

"Bart, he needs a doctor. Can't we take him to the hospital?"

"No. The antibiotics you gave him will do the trick. It was

a good, clean wound and there's no sign of infection. We've got to beat Tony to the cottage and he's on his way!"

"I can't leave him alone like this."

"You have to. We don't want Tony poking around places he shouldn't. There are too many things Jack doesn't want anyone to find, and this is definitely one of them. We'll come back as soon as possible. We've got to know what new plans your father's made."

Checking Dad one last time, I reluctantly left him. Would he be here—alive—when I got back?

We stepped out of the fireplace into the dark, silent ballroom, moving quietly to the French doors to check the progress of the approaching boat and location of guards before hurrying down the lawn to the cottage.

We had only minutes to separate the food items, books, and toys for Boomer and Sunny, and hide them behind the sofa. Just as we finished, Tony burst through the door with a fury, his surly face made more menacing by the perpetual scowl there.

"Here's Mr. Sunshine himself! What good news do you bring, Tony?"

"Have you found them kids yet? And what they took from me?"

"We're catching up on old times. We'll look later. Did you reach Mitch?"

"Can't find her!" Tony spat out the words contemptuously.

"You could fly over and find her yourself."

"I got my hands full, but you could."

"Leave my assignments? Sorry, Tony. If you're not happy with how it's going, do it yourself. You'd better get back and guide Mitch, since he's not capable of operating without step-by-step instructions. Wait. I brought you something.

Sweets for the sweet." Bart threw a bag of candy at him.

Tony fumed. "You can't brush me off. I want those kids and them stones now!" He reached for the gun tucked under his belt, but out of nowhere Bart produced a knife whose point he thrust against Tony's offending hand. With his other hand, he opened the door.

"A fond farewell, my boy. Fond, because it is farewell. Get your carcass back on that ship and keep track of your end of things. I'll handle my end very nicely without your help. Don't come back until you've got good news."

Bart backed him out the door with the knife at this throat. I let out a long sigh of relief. It was premature.

Chapter Nine

Bart returned, without Tony, but with a creature draped around him like an insatiable squid. It had bare feet and long legs, one of which kept wrapping itself intimately around Bart's leg. The briefest pair of shorts I'd ever seen attempted, without much success, to cover a shapely fanny, and a skimpy knit tube top revealed more than it concealed of two ample breasts, which this creature rubbed with relish against Bart as she moved.

Bright red hair frizzed out of a ponytail that tickled a tattooed dragon rippling across a sun-browned shoulder and back. She obviously knew Bart well.

"I'd like you to meet Kip, one of the crew. Kip, this is Allison, my fiancée."

Kip never missed a stroke caressing Bart as she assessed me. Apparently she didn't seem too threatened by what she saw. She didn't let go.

Flashing my phoniest smile, I advanced on her like a tiger with threatened cubs, grabbing the hand that stroked Bart's cheek and shook it vigorously.

"I'm happy to meet you, Kip. I'm sure you've taken good care of Bart, but I'm here now, so I'll take over." I peeled her off Bart and spun her around.

"Let me see that magnificent dragon on your back." Grabbing her frizzy dyed ponytail, I yanked it out of the way, to get a better look, of course.

"Amazing. You'll have to show me the rest of your body art sometime. Right now you're going to have to hurry to get on that ship with Tony. You wouldn't want to swim back and you can't stay here."

I shoved her out the door, slamming it furiously behind her. Then I turned on Bart.

"I'll make sure they really are going back to the ship while you gather our packages." He escaped out the back door, making no attempt to hide his glee at my obvious jealousy.

Tony had departed for the ship. With our purchases from that afternoon, we slipped into the night to the General.

Sunny flung herself into my arms. "I thought we'd never see you again," she cried.

"I promise Tony won't hurt us, and Bart's going to help me keep that promise."

Boomer's breath exploded from him in disbelief. Bart stepped out of the black night and whispered, "Dinner, anyone?"

Boomer leaned over. "Are you his prisoner, like us?"

"Bart is the best friend I told you about. He's on our side," I assured him.

Bart said, "You have blankets and food and can drink from the creek. Here's something to entertain you until we can get you home again. Stay in this tree, out of sight. If Tony finds you, you know what he'll do."

I gave Sunny a hug, told Boomer to take good care of her, then scooted them back up the tree with their bundles.

"This should be over in a day or two. Stay here until we come for you."

Secure in their assurances that they would be obedient and careful, we left them, hoping we hadn't made a mistake in revealing Bart's double role to Boomer and Sunny.

Slipping through the French doors, we stopped in a dark corner of the ballroom, listening. All was quiet. We returned to the communication center via the gold peacock with emerald elevator button eyes. Dad was awake, but weak with fever and in a great deal of pain.

"Allison, sit by me. I'm sorry we had to involve you in this mess, but I need you to do something else very important. Go with Bart to Greece and get your mother before Mitch finds her." He closed his piercing gray eyes. "I've scribbled people, places, and passwords you'll need to reach her on this piece of paper. She'll remain hidden unless I go—or you do—and I can't."

"Dad, if Tony finds Sunny and Boomer. . . ." I shuddered at the thought.

"Where are the kids?"

"In the General with blankets and food, but . . ."

"They'll be fine. I'll check on them later." Dad turned to Bart.

"Leave immediately for LAX. You have reservations to Athens at 10:00 p.m. Both of you memorize the information on that paper, then destroy it. Allison, pull Mitch's file, learn his face, his Greek team, and whatever else we have on him. Avoid him."

He addressed Bart while I hurried to find the files. I was astonished at the first file under M—MARGO! Had she been an agent? Suspect in a case? Or was this the investigation of her disappearance?

"Find it?" Dad called. Shoving "Margo" back, I pulled the Mitchum file and thrusting it at Bart, turned to Dad. Before I could speak, he said, "I don't have to tell you the danger your mother's in. Those men are totally ruthless. Be careful. You'll just make that flight if you leave right now. Go!"

While I changed into slacks and sweater and stuffed some clothes into a bag, Bart scribbled a note to satisfy Tony and left it on the table. In no time, we were speeding south on 101 to Los Angeles International Airport.

"Bart, what about your clothes?"

"No time. I'll pick up something in Athens. Read your dad's notes."

I strained to decipher the scrawl by dim map light, reading the names and places silently, remembering the car was bugged.

"He wasn't kidding when he said he'd scribbled this."

"Do you recognize any of the things he's listed?"

"Yes." I turned up the radio and whispered my reply close to Bart's ear. "I'm familiar with the islands, and some of the names. They're people we've met or stayed with while Mom did her research. The passwords are lyrics from Greek songs I learned as a child."

"Do you remember everything on that paper?"

"Yes."

"Well enough to destroy it?"

"Yes."

"Tear it into tiny pieces and throw them out the window."

"That's littering."

"Then tear it into tiny pieces and eat it."

I threw the scraps out the window, then settled back to think about my father. To see him face to face was a dream fulfilled. To leave him was devastating. What condition would he be in when we returned? What if we didn't find Mom before someone else did? To have both my parents in such jeopardy, and seemingly dependent on me for their very lives, was frightening and overwhelming. What if I failed? I couldn't stand to lose them, especially through my own insufficiency.

Making our plane with minutes to spare, we settled breathlessly into our seats. I watched the lights of Los Angeles fade into the dark Mohave Desert. Bart must have been exhausted. He was asleep when I turned back from the window. I reclined my seat, and joined him.

At JFK we raced across the terminal, barely making our connection from New York to Athens. I turned to Bart as soon as we were under way. "Can I have some answers now?"

"Okay, Princess. Fire away."

"How did you get hooked up with Dad?"

"I met him at Margo's."

"How?"

"I was trimming shrubs for my dad when this man came out of nowhere. He greeted me by name, said he'd known my folks for years and asked about my plans after graduation from UCSB. He arranged some tests, and when I passed, he offered me a job."

"How did you know it was my father?"

"I didn't. I'd finished my training before I discovered he was not only your father, but the head of an elite group with Interpol, and something of a legend to my instructors who knew him. One who'd worked with Jack told incredible stories of his escapades."

"I want to hear them all. Later. Next question. How did you get involved with the kidnappers?"

Bart's long pause told me he was weighing how much he could or should tell me. "This is a drug cartel that's been financing the terrorist group your father infiltrated. He was ready to pull the plug on the group when Tony surfaced with Boomer and Sunny. Jack couldn't demand they be returned as that would cast suspicion on him, so he played along with the kidnapping and ransom demand. Tony's the muscle behind the drug money, a flunky for the big man they're after."

"What about Sunny and Boomer's family? They must be frantic!"

"Your father has friends in nearly every government in the world since he's saved the life of almost every head of state from terrorists at one time or another in the last twenty years. The king and queen were assured their grandchildren would be returned safely."

"How do Mom and I figure in all of this?"

His answer was apologetic. "Sorry. That your dad will have to explain. Next?"

"Who is Margo?"

"The lady who owns the home you live in."

"Tell me something I don't know. Is she still alive? Where is she? How is she involved in our 'wedding'?"

"Yes, she's alive, and she had to go in hiding."

"Hiding from whom? How do you know?"

"She's part of a case your dad's been involved with. Next question."

"Why can't you tell me?"

"It's not my place."

"Have you ever been to Greece?"

"No."

"What happens when we get to Athens?"

"We meet the Grecian head of operations who'll give us our instructions."

"Bart, is Mom okay?"

"I think so, Princess. If she got your message and left immediately, I don't think they could find her. She's a pretty resourceful lady. Remember how the underground operated during the war? There's a similar underground now with some of the old timers still in place."

"But how would she know . . . ?"

"Margaret's been in touch with your father all these years."

I was stunned. I stared at Bart in disbelief. He was serious.

"Why haven't I known?"

"Certain drugs can be administered so that when questioned, you have no control over your responses. In the event you ever fell into the wrong hands, you couldn't know anything about your father still being alive."

"Is Mom involved, too?"

"I'm not sure to what extent, but, yes."

This was too incredible to absorb. Was Mom working with Dad all the time I thought she was researching in those intriguing places? Had our travels been as much for Interpol as for the University? I closed my eyes and tried to sort out all I'd just heard.

"Allison? Are you asleep?"

I opened my eyes.

"Remember our long philosophical discussions about life? Where we came from, why we're here, and where we go after this life?"

"Yes."

"I found the answers."

The stewardess approached and asked Bart to be a door monitor at the escape hatch since we were seated in the front row next to the hatch. When she finished showing him what his duties were, I turned to him.

"You were saying?"

Just then another stewardess came with snacks.

"I'll tell you later, when we don't have so many interruptions. It's not a casual topic."

I sank into an exhausted sleep soon after, mulling over the

revelation Bart made about finding answers we'd sought years ago. Where had he found them? What were they? I was anxious to hear. But I woke just before landing and there was no time. With relief, I exited the plane under the warm, sunny skies of Athens, stiff and sore from so much sitting. Our only luggage was my small carry-on, so we whipped through customs and went directly to a snack bar at the entrance to the airport. Bart ordered two tall juices over ice and bought a newspaper. We took a tiny table and I watched people while Bart absorbed his newspaper.

"Aren't you supposed to be watching for somebody . . . or something?"

"He'll find us. We'll wait."

Several taxi drivers waved, whistled or hollered. Then one stepped forward, giving a wide grin and a two-fingered salute.

"Taxi, mister? Sightseeing? I am Stavros—best tour guide in all of Athens."

He picked up my bag and headed for his taxi. Bart gently touched my arm and nodded. "We'll go with him if he's the best there is."

As we pulled away, the taxi driver grinned over his shoulder.

"Glad you made that flight. Jack wasn't sure you could."

"It was close. Heard from Margaret yet?"

"She eluded the heavy-hands chasing her. She got the message and vamoosed before they reached the villa."

I was curious. "Why don't you know where she is? You have the network information."

"Your father feared sooner or later they'd connect you and your mother to him, so he concocted a system of safe houses, or "caves," which only he and your mother knew about. They're designed in levels. If it's a temporary "lay low for a day or two," you'd go to a "level one" hideout. As things get more serious, you'd go deeper. I'm assuming she's at the top level on this one. Those bruisers weren't kidding when they came after her."

"Is Maria okay? They didn't hurt her, did they?"

"I'm sorry, Miss Alexander. Maria's dead. They beat her pretty bad and when she wouldn't—or couldn't—tell them what they wanted to know, they . . ."

Bart signalled a stop to the narration and pulled me to him as I reeled from the shock of this terrible news.

"Maria's been with us as long as I can remember, since my first trip here with Mom when I was little." The loss I felt was immediate and heavy. Poor Maria. She died to protect Mom.

Stavros quietly continued. "I watched for 30 minutes at the airport. I'm sure you weren't followed. We've arranged for you to take a photographer's holiday with a private air service. Jack specified an amphibian. My instructions were to set you up and make sure you're not followed, not even by our own men. We're not to know your code words or the safe house locations. He left nothing to chance."

That should have made me feel better, but I'm not sure it did. I couldn't believe they'd actually killed Maria. What if they found Mom before we could? I was choked with grief and fear.

I turned to Bart but he frowned and shook his head, then leaned up and spoke to Stavros who'd been doing a fancy bit of speeding around the airport perimeter through narrow winding streets.

"You have the cameras we'll need for cover?"

"They're in the trunk. Ah, here we are. I'll get your stuff. Questions?"

He looked from Bart to me, and at my vacant gaze,

looked back at Bart.

"When we find Margaret, we'll need to be on the first flight back to California."

"Beginning tomorrow, we have three seats booked on each flight out of Athens. Good luck!"

Stavros climbed back into his taxi and drove away, leaving us with my bag and a tote containing cameras, hard rolls, feta cheese, and a bottle of something to drink.

"They thought of everything," I remarked, showing Bart the contents of the bag.

"I hope Mitch didn't. This is going to be tight."

Chapter Ten

The dazzle of blue water dotted with gleaming white beaches and green islands was not entirely lost on us, but neither was it fully appreciated. My stomach was knotted with the fear that we wouldn't find Mom before Mitch did.

Bart did a low turn over Kea, then Yiroa while I took several pictures of each island for our cover, resenting each minute it took from our real destination.

Mikonos, in the Aegean Sea, was the location of the first safe house. Tiny courtyards surrounded attractive white houses and bright flowers spilled over the walls.

I directed Bart to the village we usually visited and he landed near a quaint old windmill, a whitewashed round tower with thatched roof and twelve sticks or blades tied together to form a circle. Old Mrs. Andreades peeked out of the upper window. I waved as I hopped out of the plane and she broke into a wide grin of recognition, waving me in. She seemed as ancient as the windmill—could she be involved in this espionage business?

She was. I greeted her in the demotic Greek I'd learned as a child, politely asked about her family, then plunged in.

"Mrs. Andreades, do you remember teaching me a folk

song that goes like this?" I hummed a few notes, then sang only the code words Dad had given me.

That had an electrifying effect on the old woman. Her black eyes snapped and her bent back straightened. Twenty years evaporated and I understood why the Greeks were such a formidable foe. She appeared not only ready and willing, but capable of fighting.

Mrs. Andreades repeated the first phrase of the second verse of the song and asked, "Is that the one?"

"Yes." I was relieved. The code words worked exactly as Dad said they would. "Do you know where my mother is?"

"She is not here. She came for a night and we visited as we do when she is researching, but she left the next morning."

"Thank you. It was good to see you again." I flew out the door to Bart and the waiting plane. Mrs. Andreades called after me: *"Kardya!"* Be courageous!

I repeated our conversation to Bart while he made a low pass for pictures, then headed northwest to Khios on the next leg of our search. One down. Dragonflies of dread invaded me. Time was getting shorter.

The safe house was on Skiathos, a densely wooded, small island framed by incredibly white beaches and deep blue water. The sun had reached its zenith and shimmered dramatically on the bright azure sea as we landed near some thatch-roofed beach shelters. Trundling down the stone-strewn unpaved road were donkeys burdened with a wrinkled old man, a young boy, and bundles of straw.

Our destination was a typical whitewashed house at village edge surrounded by a stone fence.

"Mama and Papa Karillides live here. They're my favorite people in all of the islands."

I pushed open the wrought iron gate draped with fragrant

blossoms and experienced a rush of nostalgia. The sweet scent and the sun, warm overhead, reminded me of pleasant times here.

Mama Karillides met me at the door. Unlike most of the other "grandmothers" we visited, she wasn't old. She was slender and full of vitality. Her husband, Papa Karillides, had a special affection for me, spending long hours improving my Greek and regaling me with tales of Greek mythology and history, mingled together till I didn't know where one stopped and the other began. Perhaps neither did he.

"Allison! What are you doing here?" she rattled in Greek, at the same time smothering me with a welcoming hug.

"I'm on a sentimental search, Mama Karillides. Do you remember teaching me this Greek lullaby?" I hummed a little, then recited the second verse.

"Of course." Surprise flashed across her face, but she sang the first verse in a husky alto voice.

"You are searching for your mother?" she asked softly.

"Oh, Mama Karillides, do you know where she is? Is she here?" I asked hopefully.

"No, *Matya Mou.* She was coming, but was being followed so she sent a boy with a note."

"Do you have it?"

"O mi yeneeto!" She was always "God forbidding!" "It is not safe to leave such things around."

"Do you know where she went? I have to find her before anyone else does!"

"If you knew to come here, you know where to go next. You will find her, *Matya Mou.*" I was "my dearest" to her.

She kissed both my cheeks and hugged me close, then shooed me back to the plane. I was close to tears. This was a home brimming over with love where I'd spent many blissful hours. I'd been pampered and spoiled, like their own grandchild might have been, if they'd had one.

In my wildest dreams, I'd never imagine this gentle, loving couple involved in espionage and this warm, welcoming peasant cottage a safe house.

"She was here," I told Bart. "She was being followed so she avoided the house, sent a note with a village boy and left. How did Mitch find out about the safe houses?"

"Margaret might've been under surveillance and they're covering the places she frequented. Mitch told Tony he hadn't been able to find her so I'm guessing he didn't know the location of the caves."

"Bart, why would she go to each of the safe houses instead of directly to level four?"

"What was the message you gave Maria to give her?"

"That there was danger. She was to go immediately to the grandmothers—to Sybil—on the islands and stay there."

"Do you know who Sybil is or where she is?"

"No. I don't remember anyone by that name or hearing Mom mention the name. Incidentally, Sybil in Greek means prophetess."

"You've visited all the safe houses?"

"Yes. Each on a different trip, even in different years."

"Tell me about Delphi. What is the safe house? A private home?"

"No. The Hotel Olympic. Apparently the grandmother in this one is Eleni, the proprietor of the hotel."

"Do you know her?"

"Yes—we've spent a lot of time at the ruins. Delphi's main attraction is its history—it rivals even the Acropolis of Athens. It's rich in mythology, tradition and spiritualism. Eleni has spent her entire life here, as did her mother, her grandmother, and all her ancestors as far back as she can remember. They've handed down wonderful stories and verbal histories for generations. Mom loved coming here. She said Eleni was Delphi's most valuable resource."

"Tell me about the town. How big is it? Will we be conspicuous?"

"Delphi's a mountain village perched precariously on a ledge above a gorge in the shadow of Mt. Parnassus. There's a single main street through the village packed with shops and a mix of tourists and locals. We'll easily blend in."

"Margaret should have spent the same night on Mikonos that we spent in your room, give or take a few time zones." Bart gave me a mischievous smile. "How will she react to that little bit of news?" he asked, laughing at the flush on my cheeks.

It felt good to laugh. My muscles ached from tension and long hours of inactivity in planes. Bart must be aching, too. I reached over and massaged the back of his neck and shoulders. I felt his tight muscles loosen and begin to relax.

"My wonderful little Princess," he whispered as he took my hand and put it tenderly to his lips. He might as well have plugged me into an electric socket. Lightning bugs zipped through my extremities and I tingled all over before I quickly pulled my hand from the offending source.

"Don't, Bart. You don't have to pretend here. No one is watching." I stared at the emerald on my finger. "Is this real?"

"Of course."

"You use pretty expensive props for your pretexts. You neglected to tell me why it's necessary we pretend to get married. And why you brought a real bishop into it. Why not hire some actor to play the part?"

"Your dad had those answers. I can help on the last one. They checked everything we did that day to make sure it was authentic . . . the proposal, your reaction and acceptance, blood tests, marriage license, and priest. Tony had to be convinced you'll do whatever I ask."

"How far do we take this charade? We will have a last minute reprieve, won't we?" The silence stretched on as I waited quietly for Bart's answer, my heart pounding harder with each passing minute.

"Well? Bart, answer me." I grabbed his chin and turned his face to mine. "You said 'pretend to love me,' not 'marry me'!"

"I also said, 'and everything else I tell you to do.' If we haven't wrapped this up before wedding time, we do it."

"I can't do that! I can't kneel before Bishop O'Hare and God and take vows and make covenants that are false. That's an out-and-out lie. How can you ask such a thing?"

"I didn't. Your father did. Neither of us thought it would be such a tremendous ordeal, in light of our relationship."

"Relationship? You terminated that five years ago. How can there be a relationship where there's no communication, no contact? You presented what I mistakenly took for a marriage proposal, talked about forever, and evaporated. You might have been dead for all I knew. You certainly didn't care enough about that relationship to drop a postcard or pick up the phone in all that time. Was I supposed to put my life on hold, my love in the freezer, till you decided I'd be useful, then abandon everything, including a fiancé, and come running?"

Bart looked at me in surprise. I bit my tongue and turned away.

"Allison," he started quietly.

"Don't say anything. The fewer lies now, the less recanting you'll have to do when you leave again." I began removing the emerald, but his hand covered mine.

"No. Leave it. You can sort things out later. With luck, we'll find your mother by nightfall and be home tomorrow. You'll have the rest of the week to make up your mind—after you've heard the evidence. Trust me, please. You promised you would."

The quiet pleading in his voice overcame my aversion to wearing a token signifying a bond between us. There was no bond—just deceit and duplicity. I couldn't look at him. Only a moron wouldn't have grasped the obvious in my agitated outpouring.

"Besides, it's safer on your finger than in my pocket. Okay?"

"Okay." The reluctance I felt crept into my voice.

"Can we call a truce here? I'm getting vibes I don't understand, but I haven't the time or energy to examine them now. We're going into a situation where neither of us can afford to be distracted for a second. We'll need all our concentration on who is where, doing what. When we've got your mom safely back home, I promise to undo whatever I've done that's distressed you so. Agreed?"

"Agreed." He was right. We didn't need to be working through my psychological hangups when Mom's life was threatened. *Get a grip, girl. No more emotional outbursts.*

The remainder of the flight to Delphi was made in silence. I forced my thoughts to the Hotel Olympic.

The two-story hotel sported black wrought-iron balconies at each triple floor-to-ceiling arched window. Venetian-style wrought iron and glass lanterns hung out front, lighting the narrow little street. The taverna downstairs was the gathering spot for tourists and locals.

During our visits, Mom spent most of her time talking with Eleni, recording stories and songs of the area, or examining the ruins on the hillsides. Therefore, so did I.

"That must be a good thought. You're looking contented." I looked up to see Bart smiling at me.

"Just remembering stories Eleni told Mom. I love the one where Zeus released two eagles from opposite ends of the world and they met at Delphi, marking it as the center of the earth. A conical stone—they call it the naval stone—marked the spot. It's now in their museum. Did you know the Greek gods revealed their will to humans through oracles, and the Oracle of Apollo at Delphi was the most important of these? Leaders came from all around the Mediterranean to seek the priestess' advice."

I stopped my narration abruptly. "Sybil, the Prophetess, would be here! Where is my brain?" I appreciated now what Bart meant. If we were entangled in emotional problems, we'd miss the obvious.

"You're right. This sounds like the place."

Bart maneuvered the aircraft in a little clearing and we jumped out. It was a short walk to the hotel. I wished it were further—it felt so good to stretch my legs!

Eleni was checking a tourist into the hotel when we reached the desk. She beamed a greeting at us. The Greeks are friendly, open-hearted, compassionate, and hospitable. Eleni was all of these.

"Who is your good-looking friend? Have you come to honeymoon in my hotel? I have a special room for lovers!"

As my face blazed in embarrassment, she laughed with gusto. That was how Eleni did everything—with gusto!

"No teasing, Eleni. I have a question for you. Remember the children's folk song you taught Mom and me when we first came here?" I hummed a little, then recited the last part of the third verse.

Eleni leaned on the desk and cupped her chin in her hand. She appeared to be thinking, but I knew she was wondering what on earth I was doing giving her code words.

"Ah, yes. Of course, I remember." She sang them softly so only I could hear. Then she waved me closer and whispered: "She was here, but Sybil took her on the hill to converse with the gods, and they sent Margaret away from the danger. Just in time. She'd been followed. Three men straight out of a Mafioso movie. They gave me *Vaskonas ofo almas.*" She waved Bart over and in a stage whisper, interpreted for him: "Evil Eye!"

Then back to me, she tossed her head and brushed her hand through the air. "I tell them *Chasou!*" And to Bart in English, "Get lost!"

"Eleni, when did Mom leave?"

"Last night, after dark. Sybil kept her on the mountain until everyone had gone."

"How did she go?"

"On the wings of Apollo, of course." Eleni laughed. I couldn't tell whether she was serious or teasing me.

"When were the men here?"

"This morning. It's okay. They won't find her," she added as she read the worry on my face. "Go! You will find her. The gods promised to watch over her." She placed my hand in Bart's, and thrust us out the door.

As we hurried down the street, I was brought up short by the most delicious aroma!

"What's the matter?" Bart looked quickly around.

"Koulouria!" I pulled him across the street to the "cookie cart." "They sell these on street corners all over Greece, like pretzels in New York and gelati in Italy, and oranges in Los Angeles. Do you realize we haven't eaten since breakfast on the airplane?"

"Take your pick of outdoor cafes. How about that one?"

"No. I just want to find Mom. We can eat the bread and

cheese we have in the plane and these cookies. There's a bottle of something to wash it down with, too." Bart agreed, although I knew he would much rather have joined the diners who were being served steaming bowls of delicious-smelling soup.

"You can fill me in on Corfu between bites." He pulled me into the airplane after him, and we took off.

I broke out the bread and cheese, and it was like a banquet to two weary, starving travelers.

Satisfied, Bart leaned back in his seat and continued our conversation. "Now tell me about the cave," he said. "Another hotel?"

"Would you believe a convent?"

He looked to see if I was kidding.

"I'm serious, Bart. You've heard of Kanoni, one of the most photographed landmarks in Europe?"

"That's the safe house?"

"According to Dad's instructions."

I leaned back to watch the scenery far below. The drone of the engine was like a sleeping tonic. Before I knew it, Bart was gently shaking my shoulder.

"Wake up, sleepy head. Corfu is dead ahead."

Chapter Eleven

Bart set the plane down on the strip like a kitten on a cushion. We flagged a horse-drawn carriage—more touristy-looking if we were being observed—and Bart boosted me into the seat. The red leather cushion invited snuggling into, and as I proceeded to make myself comfortable, Bart slipped one arm around my shoulder and the other around my waist.

"Allison, do you know what you're doing to me—being close enough to touch you after so long, yet not being allowed to?"

Before I could reply, he pulled me into the circle of his arms and kissed me, smothering my objections, crumbling all defenses I thought I'd built up. The practical side of me didn't have time to maintain the struggle for release before the romantic side of me succumbed and returned his kiss with a passion that left us both breathless.

I pulled away, shaken to the core.

"What happened to the truce?"

"The truce is off, for the time being."

As he leaned closer, tilting my chin up, he whispered, "I promise to love, honor, and cherish only you all the days of my life—and forevermore—if you will promise to marry me on Sunday."

He'd thrust a dagger directly to my heart. I pushed him violently away, struggling to keep from hitting, or possibly killing him!

"So that's it! To convince me to go through with the wedding, you'll resort to the lowest of tactics. Is that your special mode of operations? You're very good at it. Kip was certainly convinced."

Suddenly Bart stiffened. "Mitchum!"

"Where?"

"Getting out of a car with four musclemen in front of a hotel. How far is Kanoni from here?"

"A couple of miles."

"They're going into the hotel. Do you recognize it?"

I peeked over Bart's shoulder as our carriage left the hotel area. "No."

"Where did you stay when you came to Corfu?"

"It's been so long . . . I remember standing on the ramparts of the old Byzantine fortress, counting clock towers and steeples. The only other place I remember well was the convent. We didn't stay there, just visited while Mom took notes. I don't think we stayed on Corfu." With the appearance of Mitch on the scene, I'd been spared further emotional injury and embarrassment. Back to business.

"Should we take a fast taxi and beat them to the convent?"

"Good idea," Bart agreed. He paid the carriage driver, then hailed a taxi.

Kanoni sparkled in the blue Lagoon of Halikipoulou like a jewel, the tiny white convent of Vlaherna boasting a three-bell tower and one slender cypress. Beyond, in the bay, a few tall cypress guarded the chapel on Pontilonisi, the Mouse Island, which was nothing more than a rock rising dramatically from the clear water. Legend said this tiny island was a Phoenician ship turned to stone by an enraged Poseidon for bringing Odysseus home to Ithaca.

The panorama was tranquil and serene. I was the opposite. My hands were clammy, my face was flushed, and my heart was beating wildly! Vesuvius was erupting inside me.

Please, God, let Mom be here and be safe! I prayed. We stopped near the causeway. Nothing seemed amiss in the idyllic scene, but what had I expected? Bart paid the driver, reached for the camera bag and my hand, and hung on tight as I launched myself toward the causeway.

"Don't run. Don't call attention to yourself. Here's the camera. Take some pictures. We're tourists, remember?"

"Sorry. All I can think is this may be the end of our search." I snapped a couple of quick pictures which wouldn't be worth developing. My hands were shaking and I was quivering from head to toe with anticipation and fear. If Mom wasn't here, then what?

"I could never be an actress or a spy. How do you stroll leisurely when every muscle is screaming 'Run! Find her before they do!'"

The short walk took forever.

"Convents are not one of my areas of expertise," Bart admitted. "Do we knock or just walk in?"

"Knock." Before I could, the door opened and a sweet, gentle-faced sister of the convent dipped her head in salutation.

"Welcome, my children. Can I help you?" she asked in Greek.

"Sister, do you speak English?" Not many Americans

speak Greek and I didn't want to identify us as anything other than ordinary tourists.

"Yes. Welcome. Can I help you?"

"I have a question about a Greek hymn. Is there someone I could talk to, or could you help me?"

"What is your question?"

I recited the first verse to the hymn. "Are you familiar with that?"

"Yes."

"Could you tell me the words to the fourth verse, please?"

"As far as I know, there are only three verses."

"For some reason, I thought there was a fourth. May we look around while we're here?"

"Of course. The sisters are in town for the day. I can show you all of our tiny convent and something one rarely gets to see—our museum in the cellar."

"We'd love to, wouldn't we?" I turned enthusiastically to Bart, then looked at my watch before he could reply. "Oh, Sister, I'm sorry! We don't have time, but if we come back later, maybe tomorrow, could we?"

"Today would be better. No one is here."

"I'm sorry. We have to catch a taxi and I wanted a picture around the back—may I take your picture?"

"No, I'm sorry." She started to close the door.

"Thank you, Sister," I called over my shoulder as I steered Bart around the corner.

"She doesn't belong to that convent and the sisters don't go into town. Something's wrong here. She didn't know the password," I whispered as I led him to the rear of the convent.

"Is there a fourth verse?"

"No. The password was a fourth verse that could have fit—Dad probably made it up. Why was she so insistent that we go with her to the cellar? I had the strangest sensation—I felt impelled to run!"

I scanned the convent in the viewfinder of the camera as we talked and saw a small, high window, too high to look into even on Bart's shoulders. On a hunch, I sang the first verse of the Greek hymn—the password for Level Four. As I snapped the picture, I watched the window closely. A tiny square of paper fluttered to the ground. Bart saw it the same time I did.

I zoomed in on the window, but it was empty. Bart scanned the message, stuck the note in his pocket and came back to me.

"I think you've had your answer. Is this the fourth verse?" He recited the passwords.

I called tentatively to the window, "Margaret?" Another corner of paper fluttered from the window. As I retrieved the second note, the door creaked open around the corner. I shoved the paper in my pocket and we raced across the causeway to the main island.

A small park bench nestled among some trees afforded us a quiet place to talk and observe the convent without being seen.

"It's no coincidence that Mitch and friends have been right where Mom's been. There are too many islands, and too many places we frequented. The odds of them stumbling across the right four are phenomenal! They knew exactly where she was going before she got there."

"I think you're right, but Stavros said the sequence was known only by your parents. I don't think even the grandmothers knew which was their level. Let's suppose she's not here yet. Maybe Mitch planted our pretty little sister to catch the prize when she comes to the convent. If we got to your mom first, our friend at the convent wouldn't ever have to see her. The only entrance to the convent is this causeway?"

"Yes."

"She could come by boat."

"That's true! Oh! The last note!" I fished it from my pocket and read it aloud. "Was followed. Mouse Island, midnight. Go."

Bart whistled softly. "This helps. Either she was hiding in the convent and can slip out tonight, or she left a message and will meet us."

A terrible feeling spread through me, like pins and needles running down my arms and into my hands. I shivered. "Or this is a trap. If they know the safe houses, they may also know the passwords."

"You share a special gift with your father. You've never mentioned it, but do you also have any kind of link with your mother?"

"No. Certainly not mental telepathy."

"I believe in women's intuition. What's your gut feeling? Is your mother at the convent now?"

"Logical or not?"

"Throw logic out the window. How do you feel right now? Is your mother in the convent—either hiding or a prisoner?"

I thought for a minute, without trying to sort out clues or leads.

"No. I think somehow she got a message to the 'grandmother' in the convent and she's safe out here right now. But I don't know why."

"I agree! We'll proceed on that assumption. Next step, Mouse Island at midnight. Two possibilities: we go by boat or fly in. Either way, we're highly visible. If it's a trap, we'll be sitting ducks." Bart frowned as he thought about what we should do.

"Three possibilities. Underwater instead of on top. With scuba equipment, I could get there unseen, find Mom, and you could be standing by with the plane to swoop down and carry us away."

"I like your style!" Bart beamed, then his face darkened. "But that's a fair distance in the dark. Can you handle it?"

"I've spent a lot of time in Greek waters and I'm a strong swimmer, as you know."

"Okay. We'd better line you up some equipment. And it wouldn't hurt to find out what Mitch is up to."

I'd been watching a taxi make several passes in front of the park, and the passenger who was peering intently at the convent through binoculars as the car passed the vantage point.

"Bart—watch that taxi when it comes around again. There's something familiar about the man inside . . . and he's very interested in the convent."

We waited a couple of minutes while the taxi made the loop around the park and came again to where we could see it through the trees.

"It's Stavros!" I exclaimed.

"That explains a few things."

I nodded in agreement. "And poses more questions. Is he working with us or against us? He said he wasn't supposed to know where we were going."

"I'd guess he followed us, probably with an electronic device on our plane. What a dope I am! The question is, did Stavros come to help us, or Mitch?"

"Bart, whom do we trust?"

"No one. Too many questions and coincidences. If Stavros isn't with us, he'll have somebody at the plane, waiting for us to bring Margaret back."

"You can't go directly to the plane then. If you come with

me, we can swim away from the convent and Mouse Island, and when it's dark, you come ashore and I'll circle back to the island."

"For somebody who doesn't do espionage, you're doing pretty good, Princess." He grinned. "Let's find some equipment."

It didn't take long to locate a rental shop willing to sell us used equipment. At a boutique next door, we indulged in swimwear and a new shirt for Bart. We stashed everything in the waterproof bags we bought with the equipment and flashlights, then changed in the cabanas at the beach.

I led the way to the water's edge and stooped to don my swim fins. As I straightened, I gasped in horror. I saw Bart's bare back for the first time. Even the tanks couldn't conceal the scars that criss-crossed from shoulder to shoulder and from his neck down under his swim trunks.

I touched the scars on his shoulder. They were deep and recent. Bart stood quickly and yanked my hand away.

"I'm sorry. Are they still painful?"

"No. I'm just not used to anyone . . ."

"What happened?"

"Later." He turned to the water.

"Bart?"

He stopped, half turned, and paused, his gaze far away and filled with pain. Without looking at me, he began a chilling narrative.

Chapter Twelve

"During Tibetan riots against Chinese rule, I was sent in to quell some terrorist activities. Six months in, I was caught by an overlord who'd instigated a few actions for his own benefit. This was my final payment for disrupting his plans and crippling his organization. After they flogged me senseless, they left me tied to the whipping posts overnight, sure I'd be dead by morning. I would've been, but for some lamas who were intervening for one of their imprisoned Hoblighans. They slipped me out with their man, across the border into Nepal, and nursed me back to health."

"How long were you in Tibet?"

"Over a year. The last half I spent inside rat holes they call prisons, experiencing firsthand the intricacies of ancient Oriental torture with a Frenchman they'd also captured." Bart stopped, his eyes moistened. "Emile gave me answers, a new faith—before they killed him." He paused for what seemed a long time. "Then I was another few months with the lamas in Nepal, healing. Thousands fled Tibet, a large contingent of which crammed into Nepal. But you know that through your work at the U.N."

He turned to the water, hesitated, then pivoting slowly,

came back to me.

"I thought of you," he said quietly. "I thought a lot about you. Two things sustained me through their torture. One was the memory of your warmth, your wit, your bubbly laughter. I'd block out everything around me and run golden hills with you, swim under the waterfall, invent exotic stories to share . . . with you. Then Emile told me about his God, and I had to tell you about Him. He's real. He knows and loves us. He was there for me. Emile said even though he'd never see his family again in this life, he knew he'd be with them in the next, forever."

He stood close and touched my cheek. His fingers slipped around my neck while his thumb brushed softly across my lips. I held my breath, tried to still the sensations churning inside, the tingling spreading through me.

"I was kept alive by the memory of a saucy, smart-mouthed, college girl with emerald eyes and gypsy hair, and I wanted Emile's kind of forever for us. You know what got me through those weeks and months of unspeakable hell, besides Emile's God?"

I couldn't speak, frozen in that spot. Numbly, I shook my head, Bart's fingers still around my neck, his thumb tracing the outline of my bottom lip.

"I had never kissed these lips, these teasing, taunting lips. I begged Emile's God to let me live long enough to come back and taste them, even if it was just once."

His eyes never left mine. They dared me to move, to break the spell. My body would not respond to my commands to run. I knew what was coming, but I couldn't move to prevent it. He bent down slowly, pulling me gently toward him, torturing me in slow motion. His lips brushed softly across mine, as if he were just tasting.

I couldn't stand up. My knees buckled weakly and I

swayed, the heavy tanks on my back threatening to tip me over completely. Bart grabbed my arms, held me up, and studied my face intently.

"I've always loved you, Princess. From the time I saved you from the first imaginary dragon when you were six years old, you've been my only love. Then I found what we talked about, what we'd wanted to know." He stopped, dropped his hands, never taking his eyes from mine. "I thought . . . but I was sure wrong this time."

It was over. The spell was broken. I took a deep breath of relief and willed my legs to hold me up. But he surprised me. He grabbed my shoulders, pulled me close and kissed me, hard, angrily, then turned on his heel and walked to the water.

Dazed and confused by his words, his actions, I stood, not moving, hardly breathing. I almost believed he was telling the truth. But what about the little sister bit? What about Kip? And when he said it would be as hard for him to pretend he loved me as for me? Slowly, bewildered, I followed him into the water, my head awhirl with conflicting, confusing messages. I had a hard time concentrating on the task at hand. What Bart said touched me deeply. *What if it was true?*

Why was he so affected when he talked about Emile's God? We'd always believed in God. Was Emile's different? Was that the change I'd seen in Bart—the new faith? I wanted to hear about it. Why did other things always get in the way?

Dusk descended as we slipped into the water and headed away from the convent and Mouse Island, keeping some distance from the shore. When it was dark, we surfaced.

"I'm not sure how long it's going to take me to get to Mouse Island, but I'd like to be there long before midnight."

"Good idea," Bart agreed. "I'll take our stuff, find a secluded spot to beach, and head for the plane when I'm sure no one's watching me. I've got to refuel and de-bug. At midnight, I'll fly over the island and at your signal, land on the far side to pick you up."

"What happens if somebody's out there with a boat?"

"We'll play it by ear. The island's so tiny you can cross it on the run in a couple of minutes. I'll watch. If there's a boat on one side, I'll pick you up on the other. Good luck, Princess. I love you."

Why did he throw that in? It sounded so casual, so natural. His standard farewell to female agents? Or did he really mean it?

Reality returned with a rush as I descended into the cold water, clearing my head. His story was a ploy so I'd continue the charade, to make the pretense easier. Other things he'd said in the past few days outweighed this last dramatic declaration.

Get on with it. You have far more important things to do than mope over a conniving Casanova.

With plenty of time to think, my thoughts were not encouraging. Questions tumbled over one another about Mom, Dad, and Bart, but there were no answers.

My mind went to Margo. Why had Bart told the newspaper she'd be at our wedding? How did he know? What interest could she have in my wedding? *My wedding—there hadn't better be a wedding!*

I surfaced on the far side of Mouse Island, away from the lights of Kanoni and the convent. I stashed my scuba equipment behind some shrubs, and kept the flashlight.

Staying close to the trees, I moved cautiously from one shadow to the next, watching and listening intently before I proceeded. I didn't want to be surprised.

The only sound was the lapping of the water. Was Mom already here? Was this a trap? Had Bart made it safely back to the airplane without being intercepted?

Stumbling into a hollowed-out spot in the sand that was surrounded by bushes, I snuggled down into the bottom of it to check the time. Ten minutes to midnight! Would she come?

There was no movement. Even the windows of the monastery were dark. The lights of Kanoni shimmered on the water. Only the black outline of the convent broke the silvery threads that streamed directly to where I lay hidden. I could have seen any boat's silhouette. There was none.

Suddenly the silence of the night was shattered by the staccato bursts of firecrackers exploding and the sound of an airplane—no, two. They started toward the island, then turned away.

A long, low, black shape slipped through the water toward me. A canoe! *Please let this be Mom,* I prayed.

The fireworks continued to explode, echoing across the water. *Those aren't firecrackers! They're gunshots from the airplanes!*

I forced my attention back to the shadow in the water. I could make out one small form in the canoe. It was too far and too dark to tell whether it was man or woman, but the occupant with the paddle was not wasting any time. Swiftly, the boat cut through the waves, straight to where I stood.

The planes swooped closer to the island. I could see the larger amphibious one clearly now—Bart's plane. The smaller airplane, dangerously close on his tail, spurted bright streaks of death while Bart twisted, turned, and looped to shake his deadly pursuer.

I forced my attention from the air battle to the approaching canoe. How would I know if it was Mom? I couldn't reveal myself until I knew the identity of the person those few feet from me. Then another noise shattered the night. A speedboat, leaving Corfu, headed straight for Mouse Island.

The slight, shadowy figure pulled the canoe out of the water and dragged it toward the trees. It could be Mom. It could also be Stavros. He was small. *How do I make certain without jeopardizing my own safety?*

I waited silently in the black shadows of the trees, listening to the shots in the air and the boat coming closer each second. Suddenly a loud explosion rocked the night. A fireball lit up the sky. I couldn't tell which plane blew up! *Don't let it be Bart! Please, God, don't let it be Bart!*

The shadowy figure approached my hiding place. Had I made a noise and given myself away?

The boat roared toward Mouse Island, its searchlights piercing the dark sky and playing over the water on the opposite side of the island, illuminating the monastery behind me. Were they looking for me and this shadow a few arm lengths away?

Then the soft strains of a lullaby—my lullaby—wafted across the night air.

"Mom!"

"Allison? What are *you* doing here?"

I threw my arms around her and hugged her tight. I was so glad to see her I could have cried!

"What are you doing here?" she repeated in astonishment.

The roar of the speedboat and the hum of the plane's engine snapped my attention back to our precarious situation. I pointed to the sky—at the remaining airplane we could hear but couldn't see clearly.

"What kind of plane is that? Amphibious?"

"Yes!"

We saw it at the same time. It was Bart!

"Grab your canoe," I commanded as I ran for one end of it. "We've got to get into that airplane before the boat gets around to this side of the island!"

I flashed my light toward the plane, signalling Bart. We raced to the water, carrying the canoe between us, and jumped in, paddling fiercely, frantically into the lagoon. The canoe cut through the water toward the plane that was setting down as close to the island as Bart could get.

We hit the pontoons as the power boat roared around the tip of Mouse Island, illuminating the plane, and us scrambling to get aboard. Shots splattered the water all around the plane as Bart pulled us in, revved the engine, and we rose out of range of both light and gunfire.

"Mom! I was so worried about you! You, too, Bart! That was a fancy bit of flying! Who was in the other plane?"

"I suspect it was Stavros, but I'm not sure. I'd rather it had been Mitch. I still don't know where Stavros stood, but we know for sure where Mitch got his paycheck."

"What happened?"

"Lucky shot. I must have hit his fuel tank. Good thing. I was about out of maneuvers. I was sure he had me a time or two."

"Excuse me!" Mom broke in. "What on earth are the two of you doing here?"

"Call us A & B Rescue. Allison and Bart at your service," I laughed.

"I can't believe it! You're the last pair I expected to see. How did you get involved? How did you know where to find me?"

"Dad told me."

"That will certainly make an interesting story!"

"I'm afraid it'll have to wait," Bart interrupted. "We've got some decisions to make. Tickets are waiting in Athens for our flight home, according to Stavros. However, I'm not sure we should go back to Athens. They're probably waiting for us at the airport. Any ideas?"

Mom reached for the map and turned on the cabin light. "The nearest international airport is Rome. It looks like about 360 air miles. How about that?"

"Rome, it is!" Bart exclaimed and changed course.

Mom turned to me. "Your father sent you. . . ." she prompted.

"He said you would respond to him or me, that you were to stay hidden until one of us came. He'd been shot—it's okay!" I assured her quickly as she whirled to face me. "He'll be fine but he couldn't come. So I did." I hoped that was true—that he was fine.

She squeezed my hand. "I'm glad you did. When I received word to go to the grandmothers, I went to each level until I found Sybil who sent me to Level Four and told me to stay hidden until someone came who knew the passwords."

"Did you throw the note out of the convent?"

"No, but she was able to get word to me someone had been there. The sisters were being held captive at the convent by Mitch, waiting for me to show up. How they knew I'd be there, I don't know."

Bart interrupted. "We caught Stavros watching the convent. He shouldn't have had any idea where we were so when he showed, we figured he was working with Mitch. When Mitch and crew appeared at each safe house, it was apparent someone knew a great deal more than they should, and the finger pointed at Stavros. We haven't discovered how he found out."

"Everywhere I went, they were there! Fortunately, I saw

them before they saw me."

"You're a trained agent?"

"Some of what they teach you is just good sense—never walk into something without first surveying the field, look over your shoulder frequently, know who is about, and have plenty of options."

"I can't believe it! How could I not know?"

"Your father didn't want you to know."

"How often have you seen Dad?"

"Every time I gave a lecture somewhere, and other times in between."

"I don't understand."

"You've seen him, too. The 'sponsor' the universities sent to escort and guide us and make our arrangements as we traveled—that was your father, in every case. One of his special talents is the ability to become someone else instantly. He's a master of disguise."

"Why didn't you tell me?"

"We couldn't, honey. I'm sorry. Your father insisted that you be totally innocent of all this. You couldn't have any knowledge that you might inadvertently give away or that . . . her voice faltered, "someone could wrest from you if they tried."

"I can't believe this has been going on for years! How could I have been so blind?"

Mom reached out and hugged me. "It was so important that your father be allowed to continue his work."

"Mom, why do they want you? What was so important they'd kill Maria for it?"

"Oh, no!"

"I'm sorry. I thought you knew." I paused to throw my arms around Mom. "What is it you have they want so badly? Were you being a courier again? I understand you did that even when I was with you."

"Not often, but I did. That wasn't why they wanted me this time."

"Then why?"

The light in the cockpit wasn't good, but it was enough to see Mom and Bart exchange questioning glances.

"I haven't had time to tell her and neither did Jack. Everything happened too fast. And there's something else. There is a wedding planned . . . for Sunday."

Mom turned sharply to Bart. Tension crackled in the cockpit. "Is there a special reason for such a hurried wedding?" she asked slowly, deliberately.

"Margo's coming back."

Mom's reaction was a deep intake of breath, then silence.

"Jack's ready to wrap up the organization and deliver it to the authorities before they receive this new money. By bringing Margo home, we pull the money man out in the open, grab him and his organization, and put a stop to the mindless killing this group has done for twenty years. We're that close now."

"Margo is the bait?"

"Margo . . . and Allison," Bart said quietly.

"That's what I was afraid of."

"You know he wouldn't put Allison in jeopardy if he didn't feel every confidence in his ability to protect her completely."

"You say he was shot?"

"Yes."

"And he can still offer that protection? Even if he couldn't protect himself?"

"Yes." Bart said it with certainty. "Do you trust his abilities, Margaret?"

There was a pregnant pause. "Yes."

"Do you trust his instincts?"

"Yes."

"Will you go along with this?"

"Yes," Mom said, her voice weary with resignation. "Let me guess at the plan. You announce the wedding for Sunday. The cartel will do their darndest to get the mother of the bride and Margo out of the way, leaving Allison as the heir apparent, who is now conveniently married to Bart, who just incidently is a member of the organization. Very cozy."

"Heir!" I protested. "To what?"

"Margo's fortune. Suppose that, having no heir, she left her estate to the faithful managers. That would make us wealthy beyond measure. That's the carrot you're dangling, right?"

"You can see the logic of this, can't you?" Bart asked Mom.

"Isn't an actual wedding taking it a little too far? You aren't really planning to go through with it, are you?"

"Do you object to me as husband material for Allison? What does Milton J. Hollingsworth, III, have that I don't? Besides a few million dollars."

"For starters, my trust—and respect," I interjected acidly. Bart had no reply.

"Mom, I'm ready for some answers. I'm tired to death of questions."

"You're right. We have four hours. Where should we start?"

"I think the beginning is a good place."

"Where's the beginning? It goes back so far."

"Start with Margo. Who is she?"

"Ahh, Margo. I'll tell you about Margo and how she came to build her spectacular home." Mom settled back in her seat and started the narrative I'd waited so long to hear.

Chapter Thirteen

"Margo worked very hard at being beautiful and charming, and she parlayed her talents into a successful movie career. She made thirty-seven movies, wrote her own scripts, and made her own deals. She made more money than she could spend and was adored by fans the world over. Her movies were fresh, fun, full of music, laughter, and love. They made people forget their problems, and the war, for a couple of hours. The Vietnam war was at its peak then.

"Margo knew her glory would be fleeting and decided to build something that would last—something very special. She contacted M.I.T. and other prestigious schools looking for the most talented, most imaginative engineer they knew. She wanted the best. Everyone agreed on one person, but he was in Vietnam with special services. Margo contacted him.

"He was intrigued by the challenge of what she proposed. When he was able to take leave, he flew to California to translate her dream house to paper. They worked well together and were attracted to each other from the start. She asked him to stay and oversee the actual building of the house but his leave expired and he returned to Vietnam, promising to help at the critical stages.

"Margo assembled the greatest group of craftsmen money could buy. Each worked individually—none had a set of plans that covered the entire project. The secret passageways were designed to look like hallways or closets to the builders. Jim, Bart's dad, was project manager and wired the secret panels. He was the only one she trusted, the only other one who saw all the plans. Jim was recommended by her engineer, who had worked with him before Jim was wounded in action and sent home. When the house was ready for the electronic gadgets, her engineer came back from Vietnam and they installed the sliding panels and surveillance cameras, etc.

"He'd talked Margo into one thing she hadn't imagined in her little castle—an underground vault which he convinced her to convert to a communication center for his special forces.

"As they worked together day after day, making a reality out of her dream, they fell in love. But he couldn't comprehend how anyone as famous and beautiful as Margo could possibly love someone so common, so ordinary. When the house was finished, they parted. Margo was devastated. Apparently, he felt the same. They met again in Da Nang when Margo went to Vietnam to do a Christmas show—he didn't let her out of his sight.

"He asked her to marry him on Christmas Eve and Margo accepted, blissfully unaware of the storm about to erupt. When she told her agent the next morning, he said it would be the absolute end of her career if she married this nobody—especially this military nobody. The war was extremely unpopular back home and vets were jeered and spit at when they returned to the States, even those in wheelchairs who'd had limbs blown off.

"But Margo didn't care. She was willing to give up glamour and excitement for the man she loved—the man she knew loved her for herself and not her money. They were married secretly in the chapel at Da Nang with the war exploding around them. She planned to finish the tour, then announce their marriage to the world as soon as he could join her.

"They had one glorious weekend together, feeling, as all newlyweds do, their happiness would be forever. But on her last night in Vietnam, Margo inadvertently witnessed a syndicate execution by one Antonio Scaddono. She knew—and he knew—she could identify the men involved. Of course, there was no doubt as to *her* identity. Everyone knew Margo.

"In that short burst of gunfire, Margo's life changed forever. She'd been willing to give up her career for love. Now she had to give it up to save her own life." Mom paused.

"What about her husband?" I prompted.

"Since no one knew about their marriage, he introduced Margo, in her new identity, as his wife and she stayed in Vietnam with him. A little doctoring took care of the marriage records. Margo vanished without a trace."

"Did you know Margo?"

"Yes. Intimately."

"Before or after she went into hiding?"

"Both." A sad smile played at the corners of Mom's mouth.

Bart turned around. "Sorry to interrupt this fascinating story as it's getting to the good part, but I'm afraid we have a major problem. According to this gauge, we're burning fuel like a jet with afterburners engaged. We either have a leak or a malfunctioning fuel gauge, and both are sporty over a big pond at night. There's a distinct possibility we'll have to set down on the water."

"We're not close to land?" I asked, a knot forming in my stomach.

"We've passed the Strait of Otranto and the neck of land where we might've found safe landing. We're smack dab in the middle of the Gulf of Taranto . . . here."

The map light spotlighted our troubles. The Gulf of Taranto was the body of water separating the heel from the toe in the "boot" of Italy. The map established it at 100 miles across and Bart pinpointed our position—in the middle, 50 miles from land.

"What will you do?" Mom asked Bart quietly.

"See if I can raise a ship on the radio. There might be something out there."

Bart broadcast an SOS signal while I crawled into the narrow space behind me to retrieve life jackets and other equipment we'd need for a ditching at sea. The compartment was empty! By accident or design?

Suddenly Bart located a United States carrier on maneuvers in the Mediterranean, heading for the naval station in Naples. It wasn't far—a good thing, as the fuel gauge was dangerously low. He explained the problem to the radio man, who connected him to the captain. We were cleared to land on deck.

"Can we make it to the ship?" I didn't want to think of the possibility we wouldn't.

"Barely." Bart said when he'd plotted the ship's location against our coordinates.

"Keep your eyes on that area," he said, pointing into the darkness, "and watch for lights."

Mom and I anxiously peered into the night watching for the lights on the horizon that meant safety. The needle in the fuel gauge bumped against "Empty."

Then I saw it. Straight ahead several miles, lights flashed

on like power coming on in a huge city after a blackout. We cheered and I hugged Mom.

Then the unthinkable happened. The engine sputtered, coughed, and was quiet. We became a glider. Except we weren't built for gliding! We were far too heavy!

I grasped Mom's hands as Bart maneuvered the airplane to get maximum lift. It seemed like an eternity. We were approaching the lights, but not fast enough. Bart radioed we were out of fuel, and the captain ordered all engines astern to help bridge the gap—but it would take a ship that size several miles to stop.

My hands were cold and clammy. I *wished* us to stay in the air. . . . I *prayed* we'd stay in the air long enough to reach that cluster of lights. My whole being centered on those lights.

Closer. Closer. But we were losing precious altitude at the same time. Then we were there—but too low! We didn't have the lift needed to attain the height of the carrier deck. Our little Grumman Mallard plopped down in the middle of monstrous waves which crashed against the windshield and rocked the plane precariously.

The Navy was prepared for this. A giant crane—a Herculean crane—was already in place and swooping low to pick us up. Bart opened the door to grab the sling. Waves gushed in. Much more and we'd be swamped! He slammed the door and groped for the sling that would wrap the cabin, lifting us to the deck above. Just like transferring dolphins and killer whales at Sea World!

Bart was in trouble. Waves buffeted the plane so badly he couldn't fasten the sling. I went out to help and lost my footing on the slippery wing.

"Bart . . . help . . ." I swallowed gallons of salty water. Struggling to keep my head above water and fill my lungs with air, I was fighting a losing battle. The waves were winning, breaking over my face, battering my body against the plane, then pulling me away before I could catch hold of anything.

I coughed and choked on the salt water, taking more in with each gasp for air. My throat burned unbearably. If I could just get my head above water so I could let Bart know where I was . . .

Terror gripped me! Did Bart know I had fallen? I panicked! What if Mom thought I was helping Bart, and Bart thought I was safe in the plane, and they left me behind!

"Help!" It was more of a gurgle than a cry for help. Every wave that broke over my head pushed me further from the airplane. Fighting my way to the surface after each onslaught, I was tossed about like a soggy rag doll. It took me longer to find air each time the waves buried me.

Is this what drowning is like? I'm so tired . . . if I quit fighting, maybe I'll bob to the top of the water and float. And breathe. I need to breathe. Or will I sink and die? But Bart doesn't know how I really feel about him! Bart doesn't know I love him. And I never got to know my dad. Please, God, don't let me die yet.

I tried again. And again. I couldn't get enough air. I struggled to find the airplane, but it was gone. Suddenly I saw a light. A bright light. He'd come so quickly. Had Poseidon been waiting for me? Did I have a place in his watery kingdom as a mermaid with a long, graceful tail?

I relaxed in his arms and let him carry me away. We were going away from the light, down deeper and deeper toward total darkness. I didn't care. I was too tired to fight anymore.

Chapter Fourteen

I opened my eyes expecting to see mermaids and mermen and brightly colored fish of all kinds in the blue sea I'd given myself up to. Instead, there were two blue spots in a sea of white. I closed my eyes against the painful brightness. I felt sick, so very sick. My body retched with nausea. Repeatedly. Would it never end?

I heard voices, felt cool moisture against my hot skin. I tried once more to open my eyes. The same two blue spots were there, hovering above me. I tried to focus, then retched again.

"Dear Father. I thank Thee for guiding me to her in that vast sea. Please, don't let me lose her now. I beg Thee for her life in Jesus' holy name. Amen."

Why was Poseidon praying to his father?

"Allison." A familiar voice. "Can you hear me?"

What was Mom doing here? Had those monstrous waves swamped the plane and Poseidon claimed her, too? Was Bart here? I could hear more voices and forced my eyes to open to the brightness that caused such pain. The two blue spots came into focus, still hovering directly above me. Bart's blue eyes.

"Princess? Thank heaven. Margaret, she's conscious!" Mom hugged me till I hurt. I looked around. This was not Poseidon's kingdom but the ship's hospital. The bright light still blinded my eyes. I closed them again and lay back against the pillow. I felt absolutely rotten. I almost wished I'd drowned. At least I'd be beyond this wretched, abysmal sickness that engulfed me.

Mom was holding my hands, rubbing my cold arms, brushing my wet hair from my face, trying to make me more comfortable, smothering me with love and concern. I wanted to be left alone in my misery. Thank heaven Bart was gone. Where did he go?

"Will the ship's radio reach California? Dad will want to know you're safe." That's all I got out before I retched again, but it was enough. Mom was anxious to talk to Dad. Then I was alone, blessedly, peacefully alone. To be so nauseous I couldn't hold my head up was one thing, but to be observed in the process was unbearable.

Gradually I began to feel a little better. I sat up slowly and looked around the room. In one corner a door labeled "Shower" caught my eye. How splendid a hot shower would feel. My body shivered uncontrollably, whether from cold or being sick, I couldn't tell. My legs buckled under me as I slid to the floor. Whoops! I held on to the edge of the table to steady my quivering legs, then staggered to the shower.

I jettisoned dripping, salty clothes and yielded my shivering, aching body to a hot water massage. The water pummelled my shoulders, arms, and back, then worked an ablution of the sea on my face and hair. You'd think I'd had enough water—would even be repulsed by it—but this was soothing and invigorating. I would live now. I wanted to live.

This revelation was interrupted by a pounding on the

door. "Are you okay, Allison? Open the door!" Mom sounded frantic.

I turned off the water. "Are there any towels? I forgot to look."

"I thought you'd passed out in there." She found a linen closet and handed me a white turkish towel with "USN" stamped in one corner. "How do you feel? We had some anxious moments when we thought we had lost you."

"I thought I'd drowned. How did I end up here?"

"I saw you slip off the wing and yelled to Bart just as he made the connection securing the airplane. He couldn't see you in the dark. He grabbed the rope I'd tied to the plane and jumped blindly in to get you. The searchlights picked you up or he'd never have found you. He was like a madman, screaming for you, searching in every direction. You were far beyond the range of the rope, so he let go and went after you. Fortunately, the Navy had a rescue crew standing by. They pulled you both out, half drowned. In fact, you were probably more dead than alive by the time they got to you. We can thank Bart for your life, and the Navy for all of ours."

Mom handed me the waterproof bag Bart had crammed our clothes in. "You'll need these dry clothes."

"Wherever did you get this!"

"On the airplane. When we were hoisted on deck, I found it behind my seat and figured you'd appreciate something dry."

"You'll never know how much! I feel almost human again! Did you talk to Dad?"

Mom frowned. "He doesn't answer." She was quiet, her face betraying her anxiety and fear.

"What's the matter?"

"Bart's afraid Tony found the communication center and

your father. There's no one he can send in to check. If Stavros was duplicitous, who else might be? Who can we trust?"

By this time I was dressed and shook my hair into some semblance of order.

"Let's join Bart."

Lieutenant Commander Haggarty waited to lead us to the radio room, then discreetly withdrew. Bart was still trying to raise Dad.

"Welcome back to the land of the living! I'm glad to see you on your feet—with some color in your lovely cheeks." Bart's greeting was warm and enthusiastic.

"I understand you get the credit for plucking me from Poseidon's grasp. How do you thank someone who's just saved your life?"

"I'll think of something appropriate." He took my hands in his and brought them to his lips, pulling me close to him. The churning in my stomach started again. I couldn't look away from those intense eyes. Those teasing blue eyes. *Get hold of yourself. You have to be in control. He's playing with you again.* I shut my eyes, pulled my hands away and stepped back.

"Thanks, big brother! Your little sister is eternally grateful." Change the subject. "Mom said Dad isn't answering. He could be checking on the kids or sleeping. You don't really think Tony found the communication center, do you?"

Bart's demeanor transformed instantly from cavalier to somber. "I don't know. I was sure he'd stay by the radio. He was worried about Margaret and wanted to know immediately when we found her. It's unlike him to not be where he should be."

"How serious were his wounds?" Mom asked quietly,

voicing my own fears.

"Serious, but they were clean and he was taking antibiotics—some powerful new drug we've used lately that's very effective. I'm not worried about his physical condition—if he's still in the communication center. But why isn't he there—why isn't he answering the radio?" Bart asked, frustrated.

"Is there a telephone in the center?"

"Not the communication center. Margo's secret room."

Bart and I both whirled to look at Mom. She recited a phone number. "That's where I call when he's at Margo's."

Bart looked at the radio man. "Can I use your phone?"

"Sure. It all comes out of the same pocket eventually," he grinned.

I held my breath. Mom reached for my hand, then put her arm around my shoulder when she felt the tension in my body. No one spoke. The seconds dragged on and on—even a transatlantic phone call shouldn't take so long.

"Is it ringing?"

"Just started." Bart's fingers counted the rings for me—five, six, seven, eight. Then he stopped. I couldn't read the expression on his face.

Mom took the receiver from his hand. "May I speak to the lady of the house?"

She's lost it! Bart and I exchanged puzzled glances and he shrugged in bewilderment.

"Then may I speak to the man of the house?" She broke into a relieved smile. "Yes, I'm fine. The rescuers you sent did a terrific job—to a point—then the Navy stepped in. But how are you?"

I wished this were a conference call. I couldn't stand the suspense of not knowing what Dad was saying! Mom listened to a long narrative, then interjected, "Don't you leave that room!" That was too much for me!

"What's happening?" I demanded. It was a toss-up who would grab the phone from her first, Bart or me.

"Jack, I'll let Bart talk some sense into you if you won't listen to me." Mom handed the phone to Bart.

"You have a problem," Bart said to Dad.

"What is it?" I demanded again. "What's going on?"

"Ssh!" Mom whispered, concentrating on Bart's end of the conversation.

"How'd you figure that out?" Bart queried, then listened again for an interminably long interval. Patience has never been one of my virtues, but this was unbearable!

"Margaret's right. Stay put. If they haven't found you now, chances are, they won't. You have the advantage of monitoring their movements. Don't worry about the kids—they have provisions enough until we get back."

Bart paused. "We've had a slight change of plans. We're on our way to Rome. Stavros wasn't friendly anymore."

Silence on this end. If I was a nail biter, I'd be nibbling bloody stubs by now.

"Yes, I've got the code. That serious, huh? Look for us in the next 15 hours, give or take a few time zones and refuelings. Don't take any chances. Stay put until we get back." Bart hung up.

"What did he say?" I demanded.

"I've got to make a few phone calls. Margaret, tell her all you know and I'll fill in when I'm finished."

Bart turned to the radio operator and asked him to get the commander of the Naval base at Naples on the line immediately.

"Sir," he said hesitantly, "it is the middle of the night in Naples. . . ."

"Actually, Seaman Knopf, it is 03:45 and he probably has

a briefing in another hour or so—let's give him something to brief the briefer on. Now!" Bart's voice, no longer amiable, crackled with authority and the seaman turned quickly to his radio.

"Sir, I have Captain Monihan on the line." Under his breath he muttered, "And he's not a happy camper at being disturbed this time of night!"

"Thank you, Knopf. Now will you step into the corridor until I complete this call?"

Knopf stuttered in astonishment. "I can't leave my post. . . ."

"Now! I'll call you as soon as I'm through," Bart commanded, and Knopf hustled to obey.

"Captain Monihan, sir, I'm sorry to wake you at this hour, but you're the only person with authority sufficient to handle this matter. I'll give you code names and you are to call Washington for confirmation. Please make necessary arrangements before we dock in Naples, which should be within the hour. Are you ready, sir? Code name 'Anastasia'—this is Apollo speaking. Zeus is in trouble at Mount Olympus West. We need transport there immediately. I request the Lear jet the Air Force keeps at your base be ready and waiting when we disembark. I'll need you to call ahead to the Azores and Andrews AFB to alert them to immediate refueling requirements upon our arrival at each base. Do you have any questions, sir?"

There was a short pause before Bart spoke again. "No, sir. This is no joke. You'll recognize the authority of the voice when you call Washington. He'll authorize your assistance. We'll expect a car to be waiting at the dock to take us directly to the airplane. What's that? No, sir, we won't need a pilot. I'm checked out in the Lear and I have an able co-pilot with me. Thank you very much, sir, for your help."

Bart hung up the phone and quickly summoned Knopf back into the room.

My mind was whirling. Anastasia was Greek meaning "to rise again." There was always a reason for project names, wasn't there? Who, or what, was going to rise again—or had? Zeus was, of course, the head god, and Apollo was his son. Dad and Bart. I was trying to absorb all this as Bart ushered us out of the radio room.

"We'd better find the galley and have breakfast—it may be the last peaceful, nourishing meal we have for some time." Bart signaled to the lieutenant commander assigned as escort. He led us to the galley where we ordered a hearty breakfast. I was famished. I couldn't remember the last time we'd eaten.

When Lieutenant Commander Haggarty again discreetly withdrew, Bart said, "Jack got worried about Boomer and Sunny and decided to check on them. After all, they aren't just any kids, they're royalty, but more than that, they're the grandchildren of his friend. In his weakened condition, he stumbled getting out of the elevator and hit the peacock screen. As luck would have it, Tony and Sam had just come in the front door and heard the noise. Jack evaded them, got back on the elevator, and went up to Margo's secret room.

"He watched the search on the monitors. They know someone's in the house, but they think it's the kids. Tony brought those slimy cutthroats off the ship to search the house." Bart shook his head in disgust.

Mom's face was ashen.

"I'm sorry, Margaret. He's put a man in each room to search and stand watch." Bart quietly toyed with his scrambled eggs.

"The rest of it?" I asked, recognizing his reluctance to continue.

"Tony's called in reinforcements from Los Angeles. I'm afraid we've underestimated Tony and his boss. We thought they were just supplying money to finance the terrorist operations. They're not. Antonio Scaddono wants it all. His own organization is in place and ready to take over as soon as he eliminates the big boss Kerkorian, number-two man Jack, Margo, and then . . ." He looked at Mom and me with big, apologetic eyes. "You."

I was speechless. Bart continued before I could say a word.

"No wonder he had no qualms about shooting Jack. Just did it sooner rather than later. Tony isn't the small potatoes we thought. He and Scaddono will have the world in chaos in six months."

He dropped his head and pounded his fist on the table. "We were so close. *So close.* This would do it—this one last 'situation' would wrap it up, cut off their funding and finish the syndicate, leaving the world's leaders in place—at least until something else came along. But it would take a long time for anyone to put an organization like this together again."

Bart looked at me and then at Mom. "I'm not sure you understand the magnitude of what we're faced with. This means Tony has at his command unlimited people, resources, and money. We only had half a dozen agents in Anastasia to begin with, and now we can't trust any of them. Looks like it's just the three of us."

"Four," Mom said. "Allison is a great asset."

Bart looked from Mom to me and the seriousness on his face softened into a smile. Not a big enthusiastic smile, but an acknowledgement that I could help and wouldn't simply be a burden. A major concession for someone who thought of me as a pesky little sister.

"I couldn't ask for a prettier agent." His grin broadened for a moment, then faded quickly.

"I don't understand why Tony changed his plans. The wedding was to make everything legal, Scaddono would appear and exact his revenge, disposing of the parties as planned. Why the change? Why is he trying to kill you before the papers are signed? It must be Tony. Who else could it be?"

No one had an answer for that.

"Bart, if they're calling in reinforcements, what kind of chance do we have? We can't confront them in the open like you originally planned for the wedding."

"No. Jack's working on something. We should probably come up with a few scenarios of our own."

"Can we call in the CIA or FBI?"

"Yes. Jack may already have done that."

"Sir," Haggarty approached. "The Captain would like to speak with you about the disposition of the aircraft on our deck." He was smiling. What now?

Chapter Fifteen

We followed the Commander to the upper deck where the Captain waited by the airplane.

"You must be a really important fish."

"Why is that?"

"I took you at your word and checked to see who you are and who you belong with. Do you know how far up I had to go to find out anything?"

"Yes, sir."

"However, I've just been informed the local authorities have a warrant for your arrest and are waiting to take you into custody as soon as you disembark."

"How did they find us so quickly?" I gasped.

"I told you, we underestimated Tony. He has everything covered." He turned to the Captain.

"Sir, I'm sure you realize how precarious our position is, and how important it is that we not be detained. We've got to get to California ASAP. The life of my chief depends upon us. Can you help us?"

"I think we can. Commander, have the handcuffs ready, please. The car is waiting."

"Handcuffs?" I asked.

With a secretive smile, the Commander excused himself to go to the bridge. We were entering the Port of Naples.

Haggarty turned to Bart. "What should we do with your airplane?"

"Tuck it in a corner. The leasing company can retrieve it."

We watched at the railing as the ship maneuvered into the dock. A passel of formidable looking authorities, leaning against three police cars, awaited us.

"Bart, how did he get them here so fast? How did he know where we were? Is he so powerful he even has the Italian authorities on his payroll?"

"Apparently I didn't locate all the bugs on the airplane. I found three and thought that was all. They listened to our radio transmissions to the ship and followed us."

"You mean, they were with us all the time?"

Haggarty escorted us off the ship, into the waiting arms of the local gestapo.

"Bartholomew James Allan? You're under arrest!"

"May I ask what the charge is?"

"Trafficking narcotics across international borders. You—and the ladies—will come with us."

The lieutenant commander stepped forward. "May I see your warrant, please?" As he examined it, I peeked over his shoulder. We all were named.

"Well, Bartholomew James Allan," Haggarty said. "What do you say for yourself?"

Bart gave him a lop-sided grin. "It's not true, but I don't guess that'll make a whole lot of difference to them, will it?"

Haggarty motioned to a couple of SPs. "Please take these three into custody."

They approached us with handcuffs. My heart fell.

Haggarty turned to Mom. "Since you're on a United States Naval Base, you're under our jurisdiction, Ma'am, and

I'm sure we'll get this all straightened out, but in the meantime, we'll take you into protective custody."

He turned to the SPs. "Escort these charming ladies and the gentleman to that car, and take them to the JAG's office for processing."

"Hey, now . . . wait a minute!" the inspector protested. "We have a warrant for their arrest. They're *our* prisoners. We have instructions to take them back with us."

"I'm sorry, sir. You'll have your chance at them, but since they're on a naval base, we have first priority. You're welcome to stick around and interrogate them after we've processed them in, but you'll probably just want to come back at a more decent hour."

An SP came forward and apologetically but firmly snapped handcuffs on my wrists. I felt like a criminal—like I *had* done something wrong!

The inspector protested loudly and Haggarty diplomatically but emphatically insisted they would have their turn at us. Right now it was *his* turn, and we would be in *his* custody until further notice. They could keep in touch. We were put in the back seat of the waiting car. Haggarty joined us.

"Where to, Commander?" the SP asked as he started the car.

"The runway, as fast as you can get us there."

Once we were on our way, Haggarty apologized. "We had to make it look good." He unlocked my cuffs, gave me the keys, and I unlocked Bart's and Mom's.

I shuddered. "I never want to experience that again! I felt so helpless! So . . . criminal!"

Haggarty laughed. "That's what you're supposed to feel. It's a psychological advantage for law enforcement."

We sped across the base to the runway and the waiting

Lear jet.

"It's fueled, and you're cleared to the Azores and Andrews AFB for a fast turnaround. The Captain ordered a picnic lunch put aboard to alleviate starvation in the meantime. Good luck." He snapped a sharp salute to Bart. "I think you're going to need it."

"We'd like to thank the United States Navy for all your help. I'm sure the three of us owe our lives to you," Mom said gratefully as she extended a hand to the smiling officer.

"I know I owe you special thanks." I added.

"At your service, Ma'am. Anytime."

We boarded the plane, were cleared for Runway One, and were airborne immediately. I sat in the co-pilot's seat and Bart gave orders.

"Margaret, you'll have to get some sleep so you can spell us. You don't happen to have a pilot's license, do you?"

Mom laughed. "Sorry, that's not one of my accomplishments."

"How about you?" He looked at me.

"No, the last time I flew a plane was when you got your pilot's license and turned me loose at the controls. What can I do?"

"See this gauge? That's our heading. Make sure we stay on it. Keep your eyes on these gauges." He pointed to the altimeter and inertial navigation systems. "Do you remember anything you learned the last time you flew?"

"Nothing that would do me any good in this aircraft, except possibly how to keep the plane straight and steady."

"Good! This is the course, this is the altitude and this is the heading. Wake me if any of those gauges change. I'm worn down to the core. I've got to get some sleep before we get to the Azores."

"Bart! There's a lot of difference between that light plane

and this jet!"

"You can handle it, Princess. I'm coming to believe there isn't a whole lot you can't do! Wake me if you have any problems. We won't be any good to Jack if we're too exhausted to think or act when we reach California. You know I'd never be able to fly all the way by myself."

One look at his bloodshot eyes and sagging shoulders and I had to agree with him. If I only had to keep the plane straight, level, and on heading, I could handle that.

Bart checked his watch. "It's 0445 hours. We should make the Azores in about four hours, crossing two time zones, so it'll be about 0600 when we get there. Wake me 15 minutes before. Any questions?"

"Lots. But you're not in any shape to answer, so they'll have to wait until you're alive again."

I'm not sure how much he heard. He was exhausted. We all were. But he was right. We had more trouble than I could imagine ahead, and we'd need to be sharp to stay alive. Had Dad managed to stay alive?

Behind me, the beginning of a faint glow on the horizon signaled the approaching sunrise. Before me was a magnificent panorama of stars. How could the world seem so peaceful up here, when down there it was falling apart?

If Dad managed to stay hidden, if they didn't find the secret room, if the kids were obedient enough to stay out of sight, what then? The estate would be overrun with Tony's cutthroats. I shuddered, thinking about those filthy men.

What could four of us do? Go around in the shadows and pick them off one by one? Such an absurd thought brought me up short. Pick them off? I'd never killed anyone in my life. What would I do if faced with that possibility? If it was another person or me? Or if it meant Mom, or Dad, or Bart's life? Could I do it? I tried to picture myself looking into the eyes of someone determined to take my life. It was one thing to defend myself against purse snatchers in Paris—taking the offense was quite another.

Scenario: We land at Santa Barbara airport, rent a boat, Mom gets us inside. Then what? Pick them off one by one? With Mom's knowledge of the secret passages in Margo's house, we could slip into each room and put the guard out of commission while he was alone. But from one room to the next, they'd hear the scuffle or a shot. Even silencers weren't that quiet. Unless we tranquilized them. A possibility?

Suddenly the sun was fully up, sending shimmering golden highlights across the water below. Big, white puffy clouds tinged with pink, purple, and gold tinted a watercolor world. I glanced at the clock.

"Bart." I shook him awake. "We're close to the Azores."

Bart stretched, checked our altitude and headings.

"Good job, Princess! We're right on course and right on time."

Mom woke at the sound of voices, rubbing her neck and knees. "I'm too old to curl up like that. I'm full of kinks and knots. Where are we?"

"Lajes Field. Time to refuel," Bart said over his shoulder, preparing to contact the tower. I opened a drink for him, gave one to Mom, and delved into the picnic.

In fifteen minutes, we landed at Lajes Air Force Base on the Azores and taxied to the waiting fuel truck. The Air Police escorted Mom and me to the control tower to refresh ourselves. Bart opted to stay with the airplane.

As we came out of the rest room, an excited babble emanated from the desk area. As we approached the desk, a guard was saying, "Sergeant Gonzales is okay. They didn't kill him, just taped his mouth, hands, and feet, took his uniform, and left him under a bush. They must've thought it would take a while to find him. Probably would have, if it hadn't been his turn to walk the perimeter with the dogs. Sergeant Jones saw Gonzales leave the barracks, but Gonzales never arrived at the kennels to get his dog. Jones took both dogs, thinking Gonzales would catch up with them. When they reached the corner, one dog went crazy, so Jones released him and he headed straight for Gonzales."

"Why'd they take his uniform?" someone asked.

The hair on the back of my neck stood straight up! "Please, take us back to the airplane! I have a feeling we're the reason they needed that uniform."

Chapter Sixteen

The AP didn't waste time with questions. We raced for the van, with two more APs piling in beside us.

"Whoever stole Sergeant Gonzales' uniform may be trying to stop us."

The van darted across one runway, careened onto the next, and sped toward our airplane and the fuel truck. Bart was checking the plane while the airman refueling the plane circled the aircraft slowly, stopping here and there to examine something. Reaching into his pocket, the airman attached something to the plane. I leaned out my open window and screamed, "Bart! Stop him!"

Bart whirled and made a flying tackle, landing on top of the surprised airman. They rolled over and over, exchanging blows under the aircraft. We screeched to a stop. The APs jumped out and pulled Bart off the airman.

"He put something on the airplane." I ran to the tail with Bart at my side, but a quick examination found nothing. Bart turned to the APs interrogating the man in Sergeant Gonzales' uniform.

"Want to tell me what you were doing, and why? And who paid you to do it?" Bart asked the silent, sullen-faced man who was sweating uncomfortably in a uniform too small for him.

"We can stay here till you decide to give me the information I want, you know."

A flicker of fear crossed the man's face. He had done something to the plane! It had to be an explosive or he wouldn't worry about staying here.

Mom wandered casually from the shade under the wing. "Allison, it's a little warm for me out here. Let's go back to the control tower where it's comfortable and air-conditioned. You'll excuse us, gentlemen, if we don't stick around for the ugly stuff."

Then turning to the man in handcuffs, she said softly as she walked by, "And it will get ugly."

Suddenly he broke from the APs and raced for the fence surrounding the runway. Two military police sprinted after him.

"Get away from the airplane!" Bart yelled. "Get that fuel truck out of here!"

We dashed for the van. An AP was already at the wheel. A freckle-faced airman darted toward the fuel truck.

"The keys! There's no keys!" he screamed.

Bart shoved me head first into the van and pushed Mom behind me.

"Hang on tight!" he yelled as the driver swung the van, doors wide open, toward the terrified airman. Bart braced himself at the door and grabbed his shirt as the man dived into the moving van.

"Hit it!" he commanded the driver. "Get on the floor, all of you, and hang on to something!"

A thundering explosion rocked the van precariously, but it stayed upright.

"Keep moving! The fuel truck will go . . . ."

It did. The boom was deafening. The ground shuddered and the van skipped across the runway from the force of the blast. I expected the heat from the fireball to melt our tires.

We stopped the van a safe distance from the raging inferno to watch. Our transportation had just blown sky high.

I turned to Bart, devastated, discouraged. "Now what?"

"Now we have to find another ride home." He turned to the AP at the wheel. "Nice bit of driving. Thanks. Will you get the base commander on the phone and ask if he can see us or talk to us right now?"

By the time we reached the tower, Bart had determined that the Air Force had no planes available we could use. Colonel Williams, the base commander, had the civilian airport on the phone and was checking on our possibilities there.

Inside the control tower, Mom and I paced the floor as we waited to hear from Colonel Williams while Bart recorded his statement, at the commander's request.

When Colonel Williams finally called, it wasn't good news. No commercial flights were scheduled to leave before tonight, and they were all full. No private planes were available to lease. No way off this island. My heart sank.

"Sir, may we have the van and driver at our disposal for a couple of hours?" A sheepish grin flashed across Bart's face. "Yes, sir. I'll try to return them in better condition than the Air Force's Lear jet. Thank you, sir." He slammed the phone down. "Let's go!"

"Where?"

"To the airport. Maybe they missed something. It's worth a try. We can't just sit here and twiddle our thumbs when we need to be home."

The charter hangers had nothing for us and a gloomy

silence enveloped the van as we approached the privately-owned planes parked in a far corner of the airport. There were a few, and most were small. Too small.

Bart strode determinedly toward a little office adjacent to the gated area. I couldn't sit still. If I could do nothing else, at least I could walk off my frustration. Mom joined me, pacing back and forth along the fence waiting for Bart. I was afraid he wouldn't be coming back with good news.

Bart emerged from the office with a dark cloud of defeat hanging over him. He shook his head. "Nothing here, either." We gathered in a tight circle of disappointment.

"I'm afraid it's out of our hands. We need some divine intervention."

I looked at Bart in surprise.

"Emile said God doesn't want us to fail. He's waiting to help us with the righteous desires of our hearts. We just need to ask. I can't think of a more righteous desire than to save the lives of three people right now. We've done all we can. Now it's up to Him."

Bart bowed his head and started to pray out loud. Mom and I quickly followed suit. I was tempted to open my eyes—Bart seemed to be talking to someone right in front of him. It was not a formalized prayer I was used to hearing, but a straight-from-the-heart plea for help to one Bart knew and loved intimately. When he finished, none of us spoke. I couldn't. I'd never heard a prayer like that. I felt like I had actually knelt at the feet of God.

I looked at Bart and was amazed to see the disappointment and frustration gone, replaced by a serenity I couldn't believe!

Just then a vintage silver limousine pulled up to the gate beside me, and a chauffeur emerged with a key to open the gate. Tinted windows mirrored our windblown reflections.

We were a dejected looking bunch.

"Come here!" a voice from the dark confines of the limousine commanded. The chauffeur held the door open, suggesting immediate obedience. We looked at each other, then, as one, moved toward the car, where a tiny, aristocratic Victorian lady reclined regally on velvet cushions. Long, thin bejeweled fingers were pale against a black silk dress. She wore her white hair piled high like a crown and an imperial air like a scepter.

"You are Americans," she said in a charming Old World accent, "in need."

I spoke up. "We're on our way to help my father, but our plane's been destroyed. We can't find another and we've no way off the island. But we must get home immediately!"

"Where is home?"

"California. We'd hoped to charter a plane, but there's nothing available that will get us across the Atlantic," Mom answered gravely. "My husband is injured and his life is threatened. We must get back quickly."

"You can fly?" she asked Bart, raising her silver-framed glasses on their ornate stem to peer at him more closely.

"Yes, ma'am, anything with wings."

"I have a plane. It is landing now." She pointed to the apron of the runway in front of us where a late model Lear jet was approaching. Excitement coursed through my veins and my heart pounded.

"Would you . . . could we . . .?" I stumbled over the words in my exhilaration. She was the answer to Bart's prayer!

With an antique silver walking stick, she tapped on the glass window that separated the chauffeur from us. She was speaking Portuguese, but her staccato delivery prevented me from understanding all she said. I caught "refuel and leave immediately." She would help us! The glass slid quietly closed as the limousine proceeded through the gate and stopped to await the approaching plane.

"I am partial to Americans. In the war . . ." there was a dramatic pause and her voice softened, "the Americans saved my home and my family, and I was spared the shame . . ." She dropped her head back on the cushions and closed her eyes. We waited for her to finish. "It is a debt I have not yet repaid. I would like very much to help you, but I must fly now—in the opposite direction. I would be glad to take you with me to Lisbon. You could find a plane there to America. Or I would send you in mine if there was nothing to take you soon enough."

The hope that rushed through me at her first words was dashed at her last. A flight to Lisbon and back would get us nothing. So much for miracles. I glanced at Bart, who remained expressionless.

"Señora, is your return to Lisbon right now going to save a life? Our immediate return to California can save not one, but three lives—and ultimately more than that. I'll buy your airplane. I'll pay whatever amount you name. We must help my husband—and two small children." Mom's soft plea was passionate and astonishing.

Buy it! Where would she get the money? Recovering from the shock of hearing this astounding offer, I observed the expression on the lined face of this once beautiful woman. She was pondering, calculating. At last she nodded.

Mom pulled her checkbook from her purse and began writing, then paused, waiting for the name and the amount. Our benefactress thrust a card into Mom's hand, and an amount that seemed exorbitant passed with a whisper from her lips. Bart nodded in agreement at Mom's glance. The check was graciously accepted.

"Thank you, Señora," Mom said sincerely. "We'll be eternally grateful for this help. You may consider your debt paid in full. I'd like to tell you someday of the important service you've done, not only for our country, but for yours. If you'd share, I'd like to hear your story, too."

Mom had said it all. There was nothing left to say but "Thank you so much." Bart kissed the hand the woman proffered, then she waved us out of the car.

"Go now. I think I will hear from you again, yes?" Her face softened into a slight smile, the first we'd seen. As the chauffeur closed the door on this remarkable woman, I felt I'd been in the presence of royalty.

The truck was already refueling our transportation for the trip back to the United States. Bart thanked the AP who'd driven us from the air base and asked him to request a fighter escort from Andrews AFB to meet us. Shortly, we were on our way home.

My first question was to Mom. "How on earth could you write a check for that amount? How did you know she'd sell her plane?"

"It's Margo's money. I administer her estate. Did you notice how old the limousine was? And her clothes? Expensive, but nearly threadbare. The chauffeur was dressed in clothes from the war era, a made-over uniform, I'd guess. Probably royalty, deposed by the war, and too proud to give up the old ways."

"But the airplane?"

"I'd guess it belonged to a son who'd done well in business—one who didn't cling to the old ways and ideas. He probably sent it for her."

"And she sold it?"

"She got a good deal," Bart interjected. "I have a question for you. How'd you get onto the guy who blew up our airplane?"

"We heard them talking about a Sergeant Gonzales who'd had his uniform stolen. It made the hair stand up on the back of my neck. I knew someone was after us again. But how did they know we'd be here?"

"The same way they knew to send their goons to arrest us when the ship docked. They heard our radio broadcast and figured out exactly what we were doing. I imagine we'll run into some interference at Andrews, too. But now we can be prepared."

"How did he beat us?"

"Probably a faster airplane dropped him in. Margaret, it's your turn."

"You know I can't fly!"

"Neither could Allison, but she delivered us to Lajes. She'll catch a few winks while I show you what to do, then I'll grab another cat nap before we get to Andrews."

I woke with a cramp in my leg and my neck, and stretched them out the way my cat did after a nap. Bart was asleep again and Mom was flying.

"Mom, I can't believe all this has happened. I can't believe anyone could be after us . . . could be trying to kill us."

"Actually, you. You're Margo's daughter, legal heir to her multi-million dollar estate."

"Me?" I was stunned. I flew out of my seat and was at Mom's arm immediately. Mom turned to finish her explanation when suddenly the airplane lurched.

"Bart!" Mom shouted, clutching the controls. "Something's happening to the airplane!"

Bart was instantly awake. "What's the matter?"

It happened again.

"We're being shot at!" Bart grabbed the controls, pushing us into a steep dive. Unfortunately, I went into a steep dive, too. As I tumbled off the seat's arm, I cracked my head on the corner of the panel.

I heard Bart's remote voice was telling Mom to get me buckled in . . . a roller coaster ride was coming up.

She pulled at me, but I couldn't move. My head exploded with pain. My eyes wouldn't focus.

The light in front of me narrowed as the circle of darkness closed in. *Margo's daughter? But you're my mom.* Then I was gone.

Chapter Seventeen

"Allison. Look at me."

Mom sounded distant, her voice muffled by the incessant thumping.

"Allison." Her voice was demanding, more distinct. "Open your eyes."

I strained to open them, but they wouldn't.

"Can you hear me? Open your eyes."

"I'm trying."

Then Bart's voice: "Andrews, this is Pilgrim 17. Hope that fighter escort's on the way. We're being harassed. Where are your boys in blue?"

I lay quietly, not moving, hoping the pain in my head would subside if I was still enough. I felt Mom buckle my seat belt and pull it tight, then I heard hers click.

A crystalline response on the radio: "Pilgrim 17, you should be seeing two F-15s any minute. Let us know if there's anything else we can do. Good luck."

Another voice: "Pilgrim 17, this is Eagle One. Understand you could use a little help."

"Roger, Eagle One. Sure am glad to see you. Swat the mosquito that's buzzing us. He's after our blood. Better yet, escort him back to Andrews and take him into custody."

"Happy to accommodate, Pilgrim 17. Our escort service is ranked number one." Darkness closed in on me again.

* *

Somewhere I'd lost time. Someone was dabbing at my face with something cold and burning.

"It's not a bad cut, Ma'am. Head wounds look bad and bleed a lot, but this one isn't deep. We'll butterfly it so she won't require stitches."

I opened my eyes to see two medics attending me.

"No stitches is good news, thank you, but even better news would be if you have something to get rid of this beastly headache!"

"Can do, but you'll have to be careful for a while. It's a fairly severe concussion, so you can expect a certain amount of pain with even the slightest movement of your head."

The young man in white smiled apologetically. "No dancing tonight, miss."

Bart's voice again. "We've got to do something they're not expecting. They figure we'll fly this all the way to the coast and they'll be after us all the way. Colonel, any couriers heading West right away?"

"It's not a courier, but General Helmsley's leaving for Vandenberg in about 15 minutes."

"Suppose we could hitch a ride?"

"We'll give him a call and find out."

I peeked around the medics to see a silver eagle on a blue uniform.

"Tower, this is Colonel MacAfee. Patch me into Amber Thirty on the end of the runway." He paused, then spoke into the radio again.

"Captain Nichols, put General Helmsley on the radio, please. This is Colonel MacAfee. I've got a trio here that needs to be in California yesterday. Can you handle three hitchhikers? Good, we'll deliver them pronto!"

Colonel MacAfee assisted Mom while Bart grabbed our belongings. "General Helmsley is cleared for takeoff. Did you need anything on the ground before you leave?"

"If we did, we don't now. The sooner we get to California, the better."

The medics wouldn't let go of my arms, even though I insisted I could walk by myself.

"Sorry, Ma'am. I know you think you're fine, but since you're in a big hurry, we don't have time to bandage any more cut heads or skinned knees—and if we let go of you, that's exactly what you'd have."

He was right. When they got me to the van and let go, so did my legs. Bart grabbed me in time to save my knees from hitting the pavement and gently lifted me into the van, then piled in beside me while Colonel MacAfee assisted Mom. I didn't object when Bart put his arm around me and laid my head against his shoulder. It was a gentle gesture a concerned big brother would do for an injured little sister. I could live with that right now. I needed it, even if it was basically brotherly.

The van raced across a couple of runways to a C-141 ready for take-off. A tall, lean man with three stars on each shoulder waited at the open doorway while boarding stairs were positioned. As we approached the top of the stairs, he reached out and grasped Bart's hand, pulling him into the airplane. Energy and confidence radiated from the man with silver hair and crinkly laugh lines around his dark eyes.

"I understand you folks need a lift. Glad we could help. Let's get this little lady comfortable. She doesn't look too steady on her feet. Make yourselves at home and I'll be back. I'm anxious to hear your story."

They ushered me to a seat and a pillow and blanket appeared. I gingerly laid my aching head on the pillow and shut my eyes to lessen the hammering in my head.

I thought of the sea. I visualized surf beating against rocks, and transferred the pounding in my head to the waves. As they dissipated in a froth of spray, the throbbing behind the bandage soothed and I was lost in the swirl of blue-green water.

"Wake up, sleepy head!" Bart shook me gently. "How do you feel?"

"Like a very long train just ran over me." I put my hand to my head and touched the still tender spot. Mistake!

"Where are we?"

"Somewhere over Utah."

"How long have I been asleep?"

"About four hours."

"Can you fill in some blanks in our adventures?"

"The Air Force arrived in time to save our skins."

"What happened to the plane that was shooting at us?"

"They opted not to return to Andrews with their escorts. They kept shooting back. They'll never find all the pieces in the Atlantic."

General Helmsley strode down the aisle. "I'm glad to see our sleeping beauty is awake. How are you feeling? That must have been some nasty bump!"

"It was, but I'm fine now, thank you, sir."

The General turned his attention to Bart. "What else do you need?"

"We've got to get from Vandenberg to Santa Barbara as quickly and quietly as possible. Any suggestions, sir?"

"We could helicopter you from Vandenberg to your destination."

Bart thought for a minute. "They'd hear us come in. What are the chances of a Coast Guard cutter putting us ashore in a Zodiak? We can come in from the water quietly."

General Helmsley rubbed his chin. "We'll have to see what's available in the area." He directed his aide to radio the Coast Guard station nearest Vandenberg and inquire if a cutter was nearby. As the aide left, the General turned to me.

"I didn't want to disturb you while you were sleeping, but we've had our dinner. You must be starving."

"As a matter of fact, I am." The pain in my head was so severe I'd forgotten about the pain gnawing at my stomach.

"I'll have your dinner brought as soon as it's hot." General Helmsley imparted a fatherly smile and turned to the galley. He returned moments later with a satisfied smile.

"You're in luck. The Coast Guard Auxiliary Station in Santa Barbara can arrange it. Since speed is of the essence, I suggested they stand off the coast and we'll put you down on the ship."

"Thank you, General," Bart said. "We appreciate your help." He turned to Mom. "Tell me about the entrance to the cave—the grotto."

"It's about 15 feet wide. At high tide, you have to swim underwater to enter. At absolute low tide, you can see the entrance if you know where to look. There's not much clearance."

"Is it a straight shot in?"

"No. That's why you couldn't see light. About 30 feet from the entrance, the cave turns left, and in another 30 feet or so it turns right."

"With the Coast Guard's infrared, they can guide us right in." Bart sounded pleased.

"Once you're in the house, have you a plan?" General Helmsley asked, leaning over the seat.

"The house has a maze of secret passageways." Mom took the floor.

The General looked surprised.

"Remember Margo, the star who disappeared during the Vietnam war? It's her estate. She designed it so you could traverse the house on any floor through secret passages and enter and exit in several places."

Bart added, "Our priority is to find Jack and then get to the children."

"Your children?" the General asked with raised eyebrows.

"No, sir." Bart hesitated.

The General looked puzzled.

I laughed. "There's a phrase you use, sir. 'Need to know.'"

General Helmsley chuckled.

Bart squirmed. "You see, sir," but he didn't know how to—or if he should—tell the rest of the story.

"It's all right, Bart."

"Sir, you've been so helpful, I feel you have a right to know. After all, if you can't trust a three-star . . ." He laughed lamely. "It's Bhumibol Adjulyadej's grandchildren."

"The Thai king?"

"Yes, sir."

"What are they doing in California?"

"They were kidnapped, sir. We hope to return the children before it gets out. That's one reason for the urgency, and our head operative is injured and alone in the middle of all that muscle."

"Is there anything else I can do?"

"I have a 'wish list.' I've starred some items and if you or the Coast Guard have them, we'd sure appreciate their use. Otherwise, could you arrange for the FBI to have a package waiting for us at Vandenberg? They'll be vital."

The General took the list. "I'll see what we can do," he said as he hurried away.

"Are they all that friendly?" Mom asked.

"Most of them," Bart replied.

"And helpful?"

"Generals are usually the easiest. And Super Sergeants. They've been around longest and know the score."

My dinner arrived. I could smell it coming. I was famished. When I finished, I wandered up the aisle looking for the rest room, moving very carefully. I was dizzy and my head hurt. In a cubicle ahead, I could hear the General and his aide talking.

"Who are these people, if I may ask, sir?"

"Ever heard of the group 'Anastasia'?"

"No, sir."

"I guess you haven't been around long enough."

"No, sir."

"There were lots of heroic stories out of Nam. An OSI group was wiped out by terrorists from . . . as I've heard the story through the years . . . Ho Chi Minh's people, the Red Chinese Communists, a death syndicate, the Mafia, whoever. They thought the entire group was killed, but one man survived. He's something of a legend. He put together an elite group—'Anastasia'—the Greek version of the Phoenix bird rising from the ashes. When something extraordinary happens and no one's sure who gets the credit, it's 'Anastasia.' He's been killed a dozen or two times in the twenty years since the war, and resurrected from the ashes, as it were, at least that many."

"So what is this guy? Legend, myth, or is he for real?"

"Legend is not always myth," General Helmsley said quietly, with a hint of something in his voice that told me he believed every word he'd recited.

We hit an air pocket. I let out a cry and grabbed the seat to keep from falling, betraying my presence. I hoped they didn't know I'd been eavesdropping. They rushed to my side, each grabbing an arm and helped me into a seat.

"I'm okay," I insisted. "The turbulence threw me off balance. I'm not too steady at the moment, anyway. I was looking for the rest room."

In the bathroom, I washed my hands and face and stared in the mirror at my ashen face. "Legend is not always myth." My father *was* real, for the time being. Unless Tony got to him before we did. *Oh, please, help us get there in time,* I prayed. I remembered Bart's prayer. I needed to know more about Emile's God. That was a real miracle He had performed in providing us with an airplane, even while I was doubting Him. My headache was abating, but something nagged at me. What had I forgotten?

General Helmsley escorted me back to my seat.

"We have a helicopter waiting on the pad and a Coast Guard cutter getting in place. We'll drop you on the cutter and they'll take you in. There's a slight inconvenience. The coast is socked in solid. Zero visibility."

Chapter Eighteen

We landed in early morning darkness at Vandenberg AFB, with a vehicle waiting to rush us to the helicopter warming up on another runway. General Helmsley rode along, wished us luck and asked for an update when it was over.

Sergeant Fanning helped us board the helicopter and handed Bart a small bag.

"These are a few of the things on your list, sir. We didn't have much time so we couldn't get them all, but hope this helps."

Within minutes we traveled from Vandenberg AFB to Goleta, above Santa Barbara. I was curious about the contents of the bag Bart was rummaging through, examining gadgets and gizmos I didn't recognize.

We *were* socked in. We could see nothing except swirling gray mist, but the chopper settled on the deck of the Coast Guard cutter as easily as if we'd had sunshine and blue skies instead of inky darkness and blinding fog.

The Captain met us. "The Zodiak is standing by as soon as you're ready."

"Thanks, Captain. We appreciate your help."

"Our pleasure. It relieves the routine of smugglers, drug runners, and rescuing people who don't listen to storm warnings. We're ready when you are. Can we do anything more than deliver you to your destination?"

"No, sir," Bart said. "I hope we can handle it from there."

"Our infrared located the entrance to the cave. They'll take you in and drop you at your doorstep."

"Thank you, sir. Once again, we appreciate your help." Then we were underway.

"It's a good thing we're coming in this way," Mom whispered. "I'd never have found the entrance in this fog."

I couldn't see my hands, literally, in front of my face, nor Mom sitting to the side of me. I'd forgotten how penetrating the cold was when fog rolls in. I was freezing!

As the Zodiak slowed, a crewman warned us to duck. The cave entrance rubbed against the rubber raft as we slid silently into the grotto.

Once inside, a seaman switched on a light. Immediately, we made a left turn in the minimal maneuvering space. A right turn, then a huge rock wall blocked our way, seemingly a dead end. Until the spotlight hit the stairs, we didn't see them. It appeared distinctly different coming from the sea than when we'd descended these stairs to pull Dad from the water.

I was grateful for the small flashlight they gave us—we were plunged into total darkness as soon as the Coast Guard withdrew.

Mom pressed the button that opened the communication center. At this point, I was too tired and cold to ask how she knew about it. "Jack! Are you here?" The little bedroom was empty. Bart switched on the radio to pick up communication from the ship, but it was silent.

"We'll hope Jack's in Margo's secret room. Then the next

thing is to make sure the kids are okay." Bart zipped open the mysterious bag. "This straight stick is a mini-dart gun. The darts are tipped with a new chemical. One prick induces immediate paralysis and unconsciousness, lasting about eight hours, leaving an incapacitating headache for a few more hours, and a whopper of a hangover for several days. Aim for the neck or head area. It works faster there."

Bart smiled at me. "Thanks to your suggestion of picking them off, one by one, I remembered this little item. Here's a weapon for each of you. A nine-millimeter Beretta. Watch close. This is how you load it. This is how you shoot it."

I shuddered as he put the cold steel in my hand. I'd taken skeet shooting in college, a sharpshooting class, and owned a gun for my own protection. But this was different.

"Anything else in your little bag of tricks?" I asked.

"Some wrist radios—remember Dick Tracy's?" We strapped them to our wrists while he checked us out on them.

Bart attached a silencer to his gun. "Okay, Margaret. We'll follow the leader."

Mom led the way. In a few seconds the elevator whisked us to the third floor secret room, but it was empty as well. I flipped on the room monitors and found a dirty-looking hoodlum with a big gun in nearly every room. The smaller guest rooms and servants' quarters were empty, but the main rooms were guarded.

Mom and Bart watched over my shoulder. "Now what?" I asked.

"The General. We'll get the kids, then find Jack."

I put my arm around Mom's waist and she gave me a hug. "We'll find him. He's all right," she reassured me. It was not a convincing act.

"Okay, Margaret. Get us out of here without being seen."

I hurried after them as quietly as I could, catching Mom as she reached to open the passage between Margo's bedroom and the library.

"NO!"

Her hand flew from the button as though it were hot.

"Tony knows about this passage. Is there another one?"

She turned to the opposite wall and opened it into Margo's off-season closet. There were two panels! I'd only found one. Mom moved clothes aside, opening a third panel, an elevator shaft which descended to the first floor. At a touch, the outer wall opened and we stepped into the foggy darkness between the house and the shrubs.

"This is your territory, Allison," Mom whispered. "You know the way in the dark."

We crept through the mist, feeling our way to the end of the house. Holding to the corner for direction, I started counting steps, half aloud. Bart found my hand in the dark.

"Just like old times," he whispered, "when we paced off the steps between rock piles blindfolded."

"Don't make me lose count," I murmured. "Forty-eight, forty-nine, fifty." I swung my foot and kicked a rock. "There it is."

We counted five paces to the left and turned. We should be clear. We were groping blindly in a mist so thick I tasted salt air. We paced off the thousand-plus yards to the creek.

"Left or right?" I whispered to Bart. He stood still, listening. No sound but rushing water.

"Let's try right."

We pivoted right, found the bridge, and left the manicured lawns. Then I could feel it, as I always did. I guided them straight into the waiting arms of the General.

"Sunny and Boomer . . . they're not here!"

Mom whispered, "It's about 05:30, almost sunrise. When

the fog burns off, we'll be vulnerable out here. We'd better get back to the monitor where we can see what's going on in the rest of the house."

We hurried back, worried and disappointed, to the dry warmth of the secret room.

"Now we start eliminating the opposition so we can find Jack and the kids," Bart said. "Margaret, stay at the monitor and direct us. Ready, Alli? Our mission, if you choose to accept, is to seek and destroy the enemy before they seek and destroy us," Bart said facetiously. "We'll start in Margo's bedroom."

We crept down the stairs and I opened the panel into Margo's off-season closet.

"Okay, Margaret. Where's our first target and what's he doing?" Bart whispered into his wrist radio. Mom responded softly, but clearly.

"There's one lounging on the bed, eyes closed, feet on the bedspread." Disgust filled her voice. "I assume he's asleep, but he won't hear the panel open either way."

"Are there lights?"

"Yes."

Bart loaded his dart gun and signalled for me to load mine. We each took a deep breath. I opened the panel. Not ten feet away, a man in dirty jeans and grease-stained shirt, muddy feet on the bed, snored softly. Bart crept closer so he couldn't miss and blew the dart, not much bigger than half a straight pin, directly into his throat. One short snort and the snoring stopped.

"I hope the rest are that easy." He brought his wrist radio to his lips. "Where do we stash him?"

"Downstairs in the wall behind the stairs," Mom directed.

"I'll take his feet. You take his arms," I whispered to Bart. Mud-caked feet were better than touching the grimy body.

We struggled down the winding staircase and dumped him in the dark passage. I slipped back and brushed the dirt from the white satin comforter, then straightened it.

"Where now, Margaret?"

"The passage you're in opens into the library on the ground floor. There's one man with his feet on the desk. He'll be facing you."

"Can you see his hands?"

"He's holding a book."

"See a gun?"

"No."

"We're going in. Where's the open button?"

Bart had his gun in one hand and the dart to his lips with the other. "Be ready. This is a long shot. If I miss, you're backup."

I put the dart gun to my mouth and, following Mom's whispered instruction, pushed the open button. Bart stepped through as the bookrack swung open and blew his dart. It missed.

The man looked up, startled, and swung his legs off the desk as he reached for the gun in his belt. I shot my dart as I rushed toward him. His eyes were wild and wide and his mouth opened as if to yell. He slumped across the desk.

I staggered under his weight as we rolled and dragged him toward the passage.

"Is the ballroom next?"

Mom's whispered answer was distinct. "Yes. Go to the southwest corner, third shelf, to a book called *No Way Out* by Kimball. Remove the book. On the shelf you'll feel the button. Facing the passage, you can exit outside to the left or go straight into the ballroom."

"Where's our man in the ballroom?"

"On the far side at the music room door talking to the

other guard."

"Facing us?"

"They're moving. Wait a minute."

We waited. Bart looked down at me.

"Okay?" he asked as he put one arm around my shoulder and pulled me close. I sagged against him, feeling his warmth and strength. I nodded. I was glad for a breather—glad to have a minute to draw courage and strength from Bart who seemed to have enough to spare. He leaned down and kissed my forehead—a blatantly big brother move. I stiffened and moved away, speaking into my wrist radio to Mom.

"What are they doing?"

"One's walking back and forth, the other leaning against the doorway smoking . . . dropping the ashes on the floor! Now he's grinding his cigarette into that oak parquet floor!"

Distress filled Mom's whisper. Cold fury seethed inside of me. I hated these men. I hated them for keeping my father from me. I hated what they had done to Sunny and Boomer . . . and that they'd brought Bart back into my life with the accompanying turmoil. Now they were desecrating this beautiful home. They had no right here!

"They're both in the music room leaning against the door frame with their backs to you. If you can get there fast enough and quiet enough, you can get them both. Go!"

Chapter Nineteen

Bart motioned that mine was on the right, his on the left. We got close enough for the darts. They went down instantly.

"Any movement?" Bart whispered into his radio.

"No."

We dragged our latest victims across the polished parquet floor to the fireplace elevator. The tiny space was too enclosed to be comfortable with these aromatic bodies. Where had Tony found such dirty, foul-smelling characters? We dumped them in the tunnel by the sea, and on the way up in the elevator, got the latest report from Mom.

"There's one lolly-gagging on the steps in the foyer."

Bart dispatched the one on the steps quickly.

"That's one, two, four, five, in . . ." Bart checked his watch ". . . fifteen minutes. Not bad. Next target."

"Okay." Mom's voice perked up a little. "Two in the sitting room. A nervous little man, pacing from the door to the window with a gun in his hand. He looks like a firecracker ready to go off. There's a fat, sweaty man in a filthy gray t-shirt who must weigh 400 pounds."

"Meet Cupcake, ship's chef. He's no problem, but the

little man is. Weasel has reflexes like a steel trap."

"Get ready." Bart and I tiptoed across the white marble foyer. "Cupcake's on your right. Move NOW!" I went for Cupcake and Bart had Weasel. Cupcake was no problem. Weasel must have heard us because he whirled with his gun ready.

My heart nearly stopped. Had the chemical in those darts worked less quickly, one of us would probably be dead . . . if his aim was any good.

We rolled Cupcake off the sofa and dragged him behind it, underneath a table displaying a huge arrangement of silk flowers. No one would think to look there.

Mom talked us through the secret passageway between the dining and screening rooms and we dispatched the two there quickly and quietly, hiding them with Weasel. Two more followed without incident.

"Next?"

"Room Five. His hands are occupied. Go . . . now!"

I twisted the handle and threw the door open as Bart leaped into the room. The dart caught our subject in the right cheek just below the eye. The gaping expression of surprise was frozen on his face for a second. I shuddered. As horrible as he was, I'd hate to blind him. We delivered him to the cave with his cohorts.

"Ready for Number Ten? He's at the window, and nervous. He switches the gun from hand to hand, then whirls, crouches, and points it at the door. I don't like this one, Bart."

"Tell us when. We're ready."

My mouth was dry, my heart beating loudly in my ears. He could probably hear it on the other side of the door!

Mom whispered, "Get ready! Gun's in his right hand. He's leaning against the window frame with his hands high by his head. Go now!"

I turned the handle and flung open the door. Bart had only taken two steps into the room when Blue Shirt whirled, bringing the gun down with both hands as he crouched. My heart stopped!

Bart blew the dart on his second step into the room, but as the man whirled the dart missed him. Shoving me aside, Bart hit the floor as a bullet whistled where we'd just been standing. Bart fired his gun as he rolled and Blue Shirt dropped to his knees, then fell forward, not moving.

"Are you okay?" Mom's voice was frantic. She could see us both down on the monitor.

"Yes," Bart hissed. "Who heard the shots?"

"Guest Room Number Three is walking to the door. He was closest. Let me check the others. The ones on the opposite hallway didn't hear, the two upstairs may have. Number Three opened the door—he's out in the hall."

Bart motioned for me to close the door. I did so quietly.

"Can you see him, Margaret?"

"No. I'm sorry."

"Damn! We need monitors in the halls! We'll wait for him." He motioned for me to get behind the door.

"Pete! Sam? Tony? What's goin' on? Hey, anybody!" He wasn't yelling, just a loud stage whisper as he approached our door. Bart gave me a thumbs up and a smile of encouragement. He could be so blasted charming! The footsteps stopped right outside the door.

"Pete? Are you in there?" The door opened tentatively, and a head and gun poked around the door, inches from where I stood. I blew the dart into his fleshy jowls. He slumped against the door, and I jumped quickly to avoid being pinned behind it.

Bart let out an audible sigh and I realized I'd been holding my breath, too. "I didn't know I was so squeamish," I murmured, shuddering at the dead body at my feet.

"No point in hauling this one down," Bart observed. "How about if we just roll him under the bed?"

"There's blood on the floor."

Bart extracted a navy and white bandanna from the pocket of the dead man, and I wiped an ugly red stain from the floor, hiding anything I'd missed with a throw rug while he scooted the body under the bed and straightened the bedspread so the corpse was hidden. Then he pulled me against him and held me close. "Are you okay?" he whispered.

I desperately wanted to stay there in the safety and comfort of Bart's arms, but I couldn't stand the feelings it stirred inside me. I pushed away quickly to separate my body from his and stop the sensations that flooded through me at his touch.

"Yes, your little sister is handling this just fine, thank you. Let's get back to work. We still have a lot to do."

Bart tightened his grip on me, his gun crushing my shoulder. I looked up defiantly into his perplexed blue eyes. What had he expected? That I should fall into his arms at every opportunity? Was he so used to every woman he came in contact with fawning over him that he even expected it of his "little sister"? I didn't blink or budge, just stared back at him.

"Allison, what do I have to do to gain your trust?"

Trust? Of course I wanted to trust him, but his words overpowered his actions and sent a totally different message.

"We can talk later, Bart. Let's get the live one downstairs and finish up first."

"That's my girl." It took only minutes, and we were ready for the next ones.

"Okay, Margaret. Where and when?" Bart asked.

"You've got two more in the servants' quarters."

"How many more after that?"

"Several."

"No sign of Tony anywhere?"

"I don't know what Tony looks like."

"Sorry. I forgot."

"Go to the ground floor in Number Nine," Mom directed. "Same plan as always."

I decided to shoot my dart, too, in case Bart's missed. As he gave the signal, I opened the door and he burst through. This time he had to take several steps into the room. The man knocked the chair over as he jumped, reached behind his back, and whipped a gun out of his belt. My dart hit him in the arm the instant after Bart's got him in the neck.

"Double whammy!" Bart whistled. As the man dropped to his knees, the gun fell with a soft thud on the carpet.

"How does the house look, Margaret?"

Her voice came low but clear over the tiny wrist radio. "There are three in the garden and one on the front steps, pacing back and forth. Will you take them now?"

I looked at Bart, waiting for his answer.

"I hate to expose us," he began, then stopped mid-sentence when he saw my face. "What is it?"

"It's Dad."

Chapter Twenty

A voice from far away, calling my name . . . two small huddled figures shivering next to my father . . . a dismal feeling of being wet, cold, tired, and miserable . . . images and impressions flooded my mind.

"Dad's behind the waterfall with Boomer and Sunny!"

"What are they doing there?" was Bart's first question. Mom's was, "Are they okay?"

Concentrating intensely, I saw men with dogs near the waterfall, searching the creek, turning toward the big house on the hill.

"Mom, go to the widow's walk and see where the men with the dogs are. As soon as it's clear, I'll try to bring Dad in with the children." *If I can.*

It was a tense few minutes before we heard her whispered report. "Two men are coming up the hill, each with two huge Dobermans on leash, heading toward the cliffs on the west side of the house. The only others are the four you know about. Bring them in now."

Can I? I concentrated on Dad, urging him to come to the house, but the message was complicated. With the three men in the garden, and the guard at the front door, he needed to use the secret door near the library, if he knew about it. Could I send that message so he could understand it and know what to do?

I talked to him in my mind, explaining our situation, his situation as I understood it, and repeatedly begged him to come now, carefully, to the secret door. Was he receiving the message?

Yes! I no longer saw the waterfall, but the rock formations they were running toward for cover.

Mom's voice interrupted my concentration. "They're coming in! They're about halfway up the lawn. The men and dogs have reached the cliffs. Tell him to hurry!"

I was. *Hurry, Dad! Hurry!*

Bart's attention was focused on the three guards in the garden and the one at the front door. He paced back and forth between the second floor windows overlooking the gardens in the back and the entry in the front, trying to see without being seen.

"Mom, progress report on the dogs!" I whispered quickly into my wrist radio.

"Approaching the front entrance—the guard's going to meet them."

"Where's Dad?"

"About three-quarters of the way."

"Dogs?"

"Front guard's leading them to the west side. They're headed toward the rear of the house. Your father has about two minutes to get inside before those dogs pick up on him. Tell him to hurry!"

Hurry, Dad!

Then to Mom: "What's going on?"

"They made it! The dogs just rounded the corner! Come on up."

What a reunion it was! Sunny jumped into my arms and held on. Dad grabbed Mom, then all three of us in a giant bear hug. It was a poignant moment . . . my family together for the first time I could remember clearly. We were laughing and crying and trying to be so very quiet.

They were wet and cold. Mom ministered to Dad. Bart took Boomer while I helped Sunny, stripping the wet clothes from them. I wrapped Sunny in the fur throw and cuddled her close to warm her and stop her teeth from chattering.

Mom gathered clothes for Dad and blankets and robes for Boomer and Sunny. Bart hurried to the communication center for more antibiotics for my father.

"Bring me up to date," Dad said as he and Mom snuggled on the sofa.

He sat quietly while Bart recapped everything. When he'd finished, it was my turn.

"How did you end up at the waterfall?"

"That was Boomer's idea."

I turned to Boomer and a wide grin spread across his face.

"I heard the dogs. I saw an American movie on television where they chased a man with dogs. The only way he could escape was down the middle of a river. Sunny and I waded in the creek down to the waterfall and found the room behind the waterfall you told us about."

"But how did Dad find you?"

Dad took up the narrative. "I'd gone out to find them and heard the dogs. I was hiding in the rocks when I saw the kids leave the tree. I watched until they disappeared into the pond by the waterfall. I thought they had fallen in so I raced down, afraid I'd find two little bodies floating in the water. I dived down a couple of times and when I came up for air, the dogs were closer. My only chance was to hide behind the waterfall. I found a cave and two scared kids. It's a good thing they trusted you. Telling them I was your dad sufficed. Otherwise, I'd have scared them to death."

Sunny pulled herself away from me to look up in my face. "Your father is a very nice man."

"I think so."

Bart and Boomer sat in the chair with the controls, scanning from room to room and as much of the grounds as the monitors covered while we watched and talked.

Three guards moved back and forth in the gardens, probably trying to keep warm in the early morning chill. Bart climbed to the widow's walk to check on the men with the dogs and when he came back, he vocalized all our thoughts.

"Okay, Jack. What's the plan?"

"It was ingenious the way you eliminated the guards in the house." He checked his watch. "We have about thirty minutes before Tony gets back, bringing reinforcements. We've got to get rid of those four so we have the house to ourselves before he does."

Bart flipped the monitor to the garden after ascertaining the guard on the front steps was still blowing smoke rings.

Two wandered through the formal garden and one strolled back and forth in front of the cabanas by the pool.

"Wait a minute! I think we're getting lucky!" Bart said. They all started meandering toward the center of the garden.

"Okay! Let's get with it. If three of us go out there we can sneak up behind them and get them while they talk."

Dad started to get up.

"Oh, no, you don't!" Mom said. "You stay right here."

Bart and I checked our dart guns and Mom pulled hers out of her pocket. "It's my turn now."

"No, lady. Let me go."

We stared at Boomer. "We play this game in Thailand. I am very good at darts."

"You know what this is?" Bart asked, squatting down eye to eye with Boomer.

"Oh, yes. I am expert."

"The dart is tipped with a chemical that paralyzes. It's extremely dangerous."

Boomer's eyes fairly sparkled! "Oh, yes. I will do this!"

Mom looked at Bart, then handed the dart gun to Boomer.

The plan was to each come into the garden from a different direction, and at the pre-arranged signal, rush forward with our darts and blow. Mom radioed their position as we went.

I discovered it had been a great comfort to have Bart at my side as we dispatched the others. My throat was parched, my mouth dry and my knees were not too steady. I was scared—as much for me as for Boomer.

I slipped out of the hallway onto the patio, keeping the big potted trees between the men and me, moving toward the shaped hedge that would be Bart's cover.

Three guards congregated at the circle on the south side of the pool where several winding paths converged.

I counted . . . twenty-five, twenty-six, twenty-seven, as I moved slowly, carefully into place, close enough to hear their words. I couldn't see Bart nor Boomer, but knew they had time to move into place. Thirty-eight, thirty-nine, FORTY! I stood and shot over the lush green hedge and got my man in the back of the neck as he turned. Bart caught his full in the face. Where was Boomer? He scurried out from behind his hedge and blew his dart right up into the cheek of his target who had whirled to Bart and pulled his gun. The three of them dropped.

"I like this game!" Boomer beamed. "Are there more?"

Bart and I laughed. How good it felt to laugh. I'd been so

tense for so long, and tension was exhausting.

Bart grabbed the biggest of the three and threw him over his shoulders. I grasped the feet of the next one and Boomer gripped the third one by his pant legs and we took them to join the others.

"Last one?" Bart asked Mom.

"Just finished his cigarette. He's wandering toward the east side of the house. If you'll hurry through the passage between the library and . . ."

"Talk us there," Bart interrupted.

Mom got us through the maze of passageways and out the door we'd used this morning. Keeping hidden behind the shrubs, I followed Bart with my dart gun ready. Boomer tripped happily behind me, delighted to have a part in this.

As the guard rounded the corner, Bart blew his dart directly into the man's vulnerable neck. We lost no time in depositing him with the others, then rejoined Mom, Dad, and Sunny at the monitor.

"What's next?" Bart asked, sounding fresh and full of energy.

"We still have two men and four dogs I'm not sure how to deal with, but they may not be our most immediate problem."

"How's that?" Bart asked quickly.

"Tony's bringing professional muscle from Los Angeles, not this inept scum he scraped off the wharf!"

"Is that why they smell so bad?" I asked.

Dad laughed. "They were a pretty bad lot, weren't they? I'm surprised you were able to dispatch them so quickly and easily. That won't be the case with the group Tony's bringing in to protect Scaddono when he shows up." He paused dramatically. "I've solved the mystery of Stavros and Mitchum. When Stavros discovered Scaddono was planning this move, he decided to move up himself. He had men waiting for Margaret to show up on every island that was a possible safe house. Covered all bases. He planned to grab her, then sell her, and me, to Tony. Figured he'd make a bundle and ingratiate himself with Tony who by then would be Number Two in the organization."

We sat in stunned silence.

"But if Stavros wanted Mom, who kept trying to stop us?" I couldn't bring myself to use the word kill.

"Mitchum. He'd been abused by Tony long enough and decided the worst thing he could do to Tony was prevent Scaddono from getting his hands on Margaret, Margo, and Margo's money. The easiest way to do that was to prevent you from getting back here. Scaddono would kill Tony for fouling up."

"So it wasn't Tony who was trying to kill us? That didn't make sense, but most of what he does doesn't make sense. Where do we go from here?" Bart asked.

"I've called in the feds. We'll go ahead with the set-up for Sunday . . . if you two are still willing."

I looked at Mom. Her eyes met mine. I couldn't tell what she was thinking. I shrugged my shoulders. I'd have to see what the real plan shaped up to be, but in the meantime, I'd go along and not rock the boat.

"If that's what you need me to do," I said. Mom nodded in consent.

"Bart, when Tony gets back, I want you to go meet him. See if everything is going according to the original plan. You've brought Margaret back from Greece for him. Is everything in place for Sunday? Will Scaddono be here? Has he found the kids and if not, why not? But no matter what he says, he won't see Margaret—or Margo—until the wedding on Sunday."

"Where's Margo?" I asked, anxious to meet this elusive person who had influenced my life so drastically.

"She'll be here on Sunday." Dad turned back to Bart.

All of a sudden, my exhaustion caught up with me. "I think I could sleep the rest of the day!"

"That would probably be a good idea," Mom said, "since you'll need your beauty rest to be a beautiful bride tomorrow."

"Tomorrow?"

"Tomorrow's Sunday."

"Oh!" I felt like someone hit me in the stomach and knocked the wind out of me.

"Are you sure you want to go through with this, Allison?" Mom asked quietly.

I looked at Bart. "I think Allison and I need a few minutes alone," he said. He lifted Sunny off my lap and squeezed her in the chair with Boomer. "We'll be back."

"Where are we going?" I asked.

"Tony isn't here yet, so we should have a few quiet minutes. You need to sort things out and make some decisions."

I turned to Dad. "This is a real bishop with legal authority to marry us. Is this your strategy?"

"Anything phony would be spotted in a minute and Scaddono wouldn't show. Do you have a problem with the plan, Bunny? We can come up with another if you'd rather not." The anxiety in Dad's eyes belied the calm concern in his voice.

If Margo could put her life on the line by coming out of hiding after twenty years to catch Antonio Scaddono, I guess I could go through a sham marriage to help. After all, it wasn't something totally distasteful. I'd hoped for years for a real one.

"Just checking," I laughed, the pit of my stomach reacting

in the old familiar way. I turned quickly to follow Bart before they could see how I really felt.

Neither of us spoke as we took the path that led down to the beach. Bart casually held my hand as we walked, innocently launching waves of conflicting emotion that left me reeling.

First the tremor of excitement at his touch, then the churning in the pit of my stomach, and finally, fear—the haunting, never-ending fear of desertion surged through me, overwhelming all other emotions, overcoming every thought, every sane argument I tried. It was unreasonable, ridiculous. *Why can't I escape these tormenting emotions and react like any normal person to the attentions of a good-looking guy? Because this wasn't just any guy. This was Bart. I'd been loved and deserted once. Only a fool makes the same mistake twice.* I vowed I would not be a fool a second time.

Chapter Twenty-One

We sat on the same rocks where this all began not so many nights ago. Now the sun was warm on my face. I leaned back against the rock and closed my eyes. I knew Bart wouldn't pressure me, but he was waiting for me to say something.

"I have one question." I turned and looked at him.

"Only one? I'm relieved!"

"What happens when this is over? We say 'I do' and he says 'I pronounce you man and wife' and the Feds swoop down on the bad guys. Will Bishop O'Hare say 'Dearly Beloved, this was all a hoax. I now undo what I just did?'"

"What do you want to happen, Princess?"

I toyed with the emerald gleaming on my finger. How could I tell him what I had always wanted to happen? Why can't adults be as honest and open about their feelings as children? We used to keep nothing from each other. Life was so much simpler. If I could believe for a second he was telling me the truth about loving me . . .

"Let me tell you what can happen. I can offer you forever. Emile told me how he knows his family will be together forever . . ."

"What a pretty scene this makes!" Tony's sneer interrupted Bart from directly behind us.

I must have jumped a foot. Bart whirled around to face him—and Kip. We hadn't heard a sound as they came down the trail to the sandy beach behind us.

"Hi, Tony, Kip. Where is everybody? We just got back and couldn't find a soul around." Kip made a beeline for Bart and rubbed her bikini-clad body against him, draping herself around him like a piece of seaweed, ignoring me completely.

"Hi, handsome. Miss me? You were gone so long I was beginning to have withdrawal symptoms," she purred in a husky voice.

"I'm afraid you are going to have to continue with the withdrawal, literally, starting now," I said, trying to keep the venom in my voice at controllable levels. "Whatever your relationship was before, Bart is my fiancé, tomorrow he will be my husband . . . and I don't share."

Kip wasn't a bit perturbed by this revelation or my presence. She reached up and ran her fingers through Bart's hair, toyed with his ear, and slipped her other hand intimately inside his shirt.

"Then I guess I'd better take advantage of today, hadn't I?"

That did it! I grabbed her arm, peeled her off Bart and shoved her. Tony grabbed Kip to save her from hitting the rocks, his lopsided leer displaying his enjoyment of the situation.

"Hands off, Kip! Today and forever!" Embarrassed by my outburst, I glanced at Bart and was infuriated to see him grinning from ear to ear. He relished the attention.

"Kip, you'd better get your nails and hair done so you can look your best for Scaddono tomorrow. Tony, I thought there'd be guards around the house, but no one's in sight."

"Whad'ya mean, nobody's around?"

"Not a soul."

"You're kiddin' me. The house is crawlin' with men. Did ya get the woman?"

"Yes."

"Where is she?"

"Resting."

"Where?"

"If I told you, you might disturb her and she needs her rest. We're all exhausted. Did you find the kids?"

Tony snarled. "No. I've got dogs lookin' for 'em, though." He reached for me. "Give me five minutes with her. She knows where they are."

Quick as a flash, Bart's gun was in his hand.

"I told you, she's mine. Nobody touches her."

"You're takin' this a little too serious, ain't 'cha?"

"I thought we were all taking it serious, Tony. Excuse us. We're off for a nap. We've had some long days. I trust we won't be disturbed."

Back in the secret room we found Mom sleeping on the sofa, Dad watching the monitor, and Sunny and Boomer snuggled down in their chair with the blanket, glad to be warm and dry after a cold night under the waterfall.

"Tony's back," Bart reported.

"I saw him come." Dad looked at me, a question in his eyes. He came over and wrapped his arms around me. "I love you, Bunny. You know I'd never subject you to all this if I didn't feel completely confident it will work. I haven't shielded you all your life to blow it away now. Do you believe that?"

"Yes, Dad. I'll be glad to do whatever I can."

"Including marrying this guy?"

"Even that. But whatever gave you the idea? What if Bart

and I had changed too much in these last few years since we'd seen each other? Didn't love each other anymore?" *That's not really what I wanted to ask, but it would do for starters.*

"There would have been a different plan. This one just seemed so totally right for both of you—and us."

It would have seemed totally right a few years ago. Now I wasn't sure. If Kip hadn't come along, what would my decision have been?

I could feel a deep, dull throb behind the soreness in my head.

"I distinctly recall you offered me a nap a little while ago." I looked at Bart.

"Yes. You could use one of those. Where won't you be disturbed?"

Dad spoke up. "Try the little bedroom in the communication center."

"What about you?" Bart asked. "You're exhausted."

"I'll let Margaret get a couple of hours of sleep, then wake her and she can keep an eye on things. I need a handle on what Tony's doing now. I want to see how he reacts to his men's disappearance."

"That will do me more good than a nap," Bart laughed.

"You two do what you want," I said. "I need some rest, then the next order of the day will be food. There are too many hours between meals in your business. Do you ever eat regularly?"

Dad laughed and shooed me toward the elevator. I was quiet in the passageway outside the communication center, not wanting to rouse our guests who were sleeping off the effects of the darts. I fell asleep immediately in the quiet little chamber.

I woke to the heavenly smell of hot pepperoni pizza as

Bart waved the box under my nose.

"Where did you get that?"

"Pizza Palace delivers. Want to come upstairs and eat with everybody else?"

"You bet your life! What if Tony smells it?"

"I ordered some for Tony, too."

Once upstairs, I found everyone else already eating. "What's going on?" I asked between bites.

"Tony can't find his men and can't figure out where they've gone. Tony, Nate, and Kip have searched everywhere. He's furious."

"How many new men did he bring?" I asked.

"About a dozen."

We devoured every bite of pizza.

"Now that I'm full, the only thing I need to make me happy is a hot shower."

Mom agreed.

"I think we can accommodate you both. Tony and his new crew have headed for the ship to look for his men. I'll escort you to the cottage where you can have your own showers and clothes," Bart offered.

"Nothing sounds better than that. I'm afraid I'll have to scrape these clothes off, I've had them on so long!" I shuddered.

"Tony's posted guards outside. They'll watch every move as soon as you step outside the house," Dad cautioned. "Hurry."

As we went out the front door into the twilight, a couple of Tony's muscle challenged us.

"It's all right. I'm taking them to the cottage. You keep watch here. I'll guard them."

Bart hurried us down the lawn to the cottage, then stood watch in the hallway outside our bedrooms.

As the hot water poured over me, I reflected how my highlight of the last few days had been a hot shower—washing off the accumulated grime of several days between showers!

I reviewed the events of those days . . . the quick flight to Greece, finding Mom, the flight to Naples, then . . . what had Mom said just before I hit my head?

"Margo is your mom." *Had she really said that?* "Margo is your mom." *I had heard it.*

If Margo was my mom, who was Mom . . . this woman I'd thought was my mother all these years? My shower suddenly lost its appeal. I jumped into the handiest clean clothes I could find and burst out of the bedroom, running right into Bart.

"What's the matter?" Bart headed into the bedroom to see what had driven me out in such a dither. Before he could speak, Tony burst in like an explosion. He had help and they all had big, ugly guns. The guards must have radioed him that we were here.

Bart pushed me behind him and leaned over the railing, his gun pointed at the men below. "Get your gun, go with your mom and lock the door," he instructed me quietly.

I tried to be as inconspicuous as possible.

Bart looked down at Tony. "What a surprise. Didn't I know you'd try something like this? Always the muscle. Always the strong arm."

Why was Bart taunting him?

"You'll have to introduce me to your friends, Tony."

"Cut it, Bart! I want those women. They know where the kids and the jewels are."

"Aw, Tony. You'd mess up Scaddono's whole deal because you're so greedy. Can't you wait for tomorrow when everything's tied up in a neat, legal package? Your boss won't like you screwing things up."

I couldn't hear Tony's reply, but saw him close in with his men. I interrupted Mom's shower, then hurried back to listen.

"That's close enough, Tony," Bart said quietly. "Don't put your foot on that stair or I'll put a hole through you."

Tony snorted. "You wouldn't dare. They'll blow you away so fast you won't know what happened."

"I'll get off one shot before I'm dead, and you'll be it. Take your playmates, and go away."

Tony hesitated, measuring Bart. Should he call his bluff? He hated to lose face, but he hated even more having Bart's gun pointed at his head. Bart shifted slightly and Tony motioned angrily for his men to leave.

"When this is over, you'll be sorry, Bart," he snarled.

"Do whatever you want after tomorrow. Until then, you keep those goons away from me and these women. That's the only way you'll get what Antonio Scaddono wants."

Tony left, but he was not a happy man. I'd never met anyone who seemed so thoroughly evil. Malevolence oozed from him.

"I don't trust him. We've got to get back where they can't get at you," Bart said. "Is Margaret dressed?"

Mom stepped out of her bedroom fully dressed with gun in hand.

Chapter Twenty-Two

The guard at the front door challenged us as we approached the big house.

"I'm glad you're here," Bart greeted him. "Make sure no one gets in here."

As the guard opened his mouth, Bart hurried us through the front door and slammed it behind him.

"Jack! Where is everyone?" Bart asked in his wrist radio.

Dad reported a half dozen men searching for the missing crew. The ballroom and music room were empty.

We raced to the ballroom and the emerald-activated elevator.

"Who is Margo?" I demanded as we ascended to the secret room.

"Margo is your mom," she answered simply.

"Who are you?"

"We've got an interesting night ahead of us," Bart laughed.

"I hope you're ready with answers because I've got a host of questions!"

Sunny tackled me with a hug as I stepped into the secret room, pulling me onto the fur throw beside her. Boomer and Bart joined us.

"Thank you for the dolphin and the book. I liked that book. Fairy tales are my favorite," Sunny said.

I gave her a quick hug. "Mine, too. Tell me about your adventures in the tree."

"We saw deer and rabbits, snakes, a hundred squirrels, so many different kinds of birds we couldn't count, and a red fox. There was a funny looking animal—the book you brought us called it a 'possum—and a coyote we thought was a dog."

"I can't believe we're sitting here chatting like a normal family with so much danger all around us! It's unreal!"

Dad put his arm around Mom. She leaned against his shoulder.

"Bunny, you take every moment and squeeze as much good as you can into it. You can't look forward to days and months and years—they might never happen. You take whatever you get and be glad for it."

"Dad, why is Antonio Scaddono such a big deal?"

"Scaddono's huge drug cartel supplied terrorists with operating money for years. He's expanding. He wants legitimate business in the States to launder his money. He's desperate to bring a son with serious medical problems for treatment that's only available here. He wants to walk the streets openly in this country. One person prevents that. We dangle bait he can't refuse—Margo—and her estate—for his base of operations and his home, close to medical help for his son."

"Effective bait. What's the estate worth?"

"Margo had several million in the bank and investments twenty years ago. The estate was free and clear. All it had to pay was upkeep and taxes, and Bart's family's salary. The property's quadrupled in value. Her jewelry, stocks and bonds, music and movie royalties, the property, and the house are roughly worth about a hundred million right now, give or take a few," Dad estimated.

Bart whistled. "Nothing to sneeze at! Antonio would think it fair payment for the inconvenience she's caused him."

"But if Interpol knew about his drug operations," I protested, "why didn't they arrest him?"

"No conclusive proof."

"I'm sorry I'm so dense, but will Margo change that?"

"If Margo identifies him as the killer, it's a murder one charge. Scaddono discovered you're Margo's heir. We passed word Margo would present you with the estate as a wedding present. Your will names your new husband as beneficiary and Scaddono makes his move. You all meet with an unfortunate fatal accident, Bart inherits Margo's fortune. A bereaved widower, Bart signs everything over to his boss, and Scaddono becomes legal owner of all he's coveted. He's rid of his nemesis of twenty years and gets everything he wants. That's his plan. Our plan has the feds stepping in as soon as he shows his face here for the wedding and he's all sewed up. Make sense now?"

"Yes . . . except where you got the idea for a marriage."

"Bunny, I thought you and Bart . . ."

I interrupted, ignoring the assumption. "Does that mean there isn't much danger to us until after the wedding?"

"You've got some information Tony wants—where the kids and the jewels are."

Dad turned to Boomer and Sunny. "You do still have the jewels?"

"No, sir," Boomer smiled. "We don't have them anymore and we don't know where they are."

Dad paled.

"It's all right, Dad. They gave me the jewels and I hid them here in the house."

At that moment, the monitor revealed Tony back on the scene with his cohorts in crime and we watched them file into the white marble foyer. Tony was yelling.

"They just don't disappear off the face of the earth! Where'd they go? First the girl, and then the kids and the jewels, now my men. I want 'em found now!"

"But, Tony . . ." whined one of the men.

"Don't 'but Tony' me! Do whatever it takes to find 'em! We need those men to make sure nothin' goes wrong tomorrow. Look till you find 'em. I want men, kids, and jewels, and I want 'em now!"

It was amazing. Tony wasn't a big man, and though some of the men dwarfed him, they cowered before him. They spread out to search again. Tony paced the sitting room with a bookish man Dad identified as his "lieutenant," Nate.

I watched in horror and amusement as Tony ranted and raved at Nate while the little man kept turning his head like he was listening for something.

"Tony, be quiet," Nate said quickly.

Tony went apoplectic! "Be quiet?" he roared.

"Ssh. Listen."

Tony pulled his gun and whirled around, examining the room. "To what? Whad'ya hear?"

"I'm not sure. Something."

"Where? In here? Outside?"

They stood still, listening. Tony examined the room, cocking his ear. Nate went to the door, checked the foyer, then the screening room.

"Guess I was wrong. I don't hear anything now."

They relaxed a little, even sat down, but they faced the doors and remained watchful. We knew what the sound was.

Cupcake!

I heard sounds in our room and turned around to see Sunny and Boomer yawning. That made me yawn.

"It's getting close to bedtime," Mom noted. "I think it's time everyone turned in."

Dad looked exhausted. "We need to keep an eye on everybody tonight. Bunny, you had a long nap today. Would you take the first watch?"

"Sure." I spread blankets on the carpet and Sunny and Boomer snuggled down contentedly. We insisted Dad take the sofa and I got the chair with the monitor controls. Mom curled up in the other chair while Bart sprawled on the fur throw on the floor.

"Mom?" I whispered when everyone seemed to be sleeping. "Are you awake?" She nodded. "If Margo's my mom, who are you? Margo?"

A smile danced in her eyes. "I wondered how long it would take you."

"But she was blonde with blue eyes. Your hair is black—I know it's your natural color—and you have dark eyes."

"Colored lenses and bleach." She was enjoying this.

"What color are your eyes?"

"What you see is the genuine article. When I made my first movie, blue-eyed blondes were in vogue so I became one. When I dropped that identity in Vietnam, I dyed my hair back to its natural color and removed the lenses. Voila! Glamorous Margo disappears and plain old Margaret returns."

"You've lived two entirely different lives."

"I was lucky. Most people never have so much."

"Lucky?"

"I've had the best of all worlds—fortune and fame, then a fulfilling career in literature and folklore. The most satisfying has been being a wife and your mother."

I hugged her.

"You're the best thing that happened to me," she said, cupping my face in her hands. "I named you Melanie Allison because you were the light that came after the darkest part of my life. Now you can understand why. I'd fallen in love with a brilliant, wonderful man as we built this house." She pointed to the picture of the man on the wall.

"That's Dad?"

"When I first met him. When I witnessed the gruesome execution of an important, influential family by Scaddono, right after your dad and I were secretly married, Scaddono searched everywhere. So Margo disappeared. I was welcomed into the circle of military wives and absorbed into that lifestyle without questions. Then you came along . . . the brightest spot in my life."

"Mom, I must have grandparents somewhere."

Mom smiled a sweet, mysterious smile. "If you could choose your own grandparents from anyone you know, who would you choose?"

I sat back on the floor and pondered. "I guess it would have to be Mama and Papa Karillides on Skiathos. They've been more like a grandma and grandpa than anyone else."

"They'll be delighted to hear that. They're my parents, your grandparents."

"What about Dad's parents?"

"They were killed in an accident before I met him, while he was still in college."

"How about other family? Aunts? Uncles? Cousins?"

Just then a movement on the monitor caught my eye. I jumped up off the floor and turned up the audio. A couple of Tony's men reported their search.

"Tony, there's nobody here. This house is empty."

Tony was a volcano of fury about to erupt. He smashed his gun against a Ming Dynasty urn. Mom gasped.

"That was a gift from Madame Chaing Kai-shek!! It was priceless!"

Apparently Nate knew the value. "Tony! That fit of temper just cost you a cool two million dollars. That vase is Ming Dynasty—it's irreplaceable! You can't swing an arm in here without it costing an easy hundred grand."

Tony brushed him off and turned his attention to his returning men.

"Where are they?" he stomped. "Secret passages, that's where. Why can'tcha find 'em? Don't sit there like dummies. Get out there and look!"

Mom laughed. "If Tony keeps everybody busy all night, maybe they'll be too tired to see the trap we're setting."

I was feeling the hours in this long day and would be glad to have it over. Why wasn't Tony getting tired?

He was seething with rage and each duo that returned empty-handed increased his fury. One ruffian, dirtier looking than the rest, came in.

"Tony, I think ya lost it. There ain't nobody here. You sure you ain't dreamin'?"

Tony leaped at his throat like a hungry jackal. "You sayin' I don't know what's goin' on around here? You sayin' I ain't in charge?"

The man backed away from Tony's frenzied attack. "No, Tony, I ain't sayin' that." He laughed nervously. "Loosen up. I'm sayin' there ain't nobody here but us. You sure there was? Did'ja see 'em yourself?"

"You callin' me a liar? You callin' me incompetent?" Tony's face was purple with anger and his gravelly voice rose higher with each question. Nate started to move up to smooth out the situation but he wasn't fast enough.

The look on Tony's face was evil . . . cold, calculating, unadulterated evil. He pointed his gun at the man's head and pulled the trigger. Blood splattered everywhere. The body hit the floor with a thud. Tony whirled to face the others, who were standing with their mouths open.

"Anybody else think I don't know what I'm doin'? Anybody else think I'm losin' it?" he shouted, waving his gun in their faces.

"I can't believe it!" I said to Mom. "He's like a crazy man!"

"He's totally unpredictable, not a bit of conscience, the most dangerous kind of man. He and Antonio are two of a kind."

Suddenly I had an insight into the fear Mom had lived with all these years knowing Scaddono was looking for her, would do anything to find her, and was now planning her death.

"Has it been awful?" I asked softly.

Mom looked at me for a long minute, then back at the monitor. "Knowing if Scaddono found me I'd be as dead as that man lying in my foyer?"

I nodded.

"There have been moments of terror when I thought he was close, but weeks and months when he was nothing more than a nightmare out of my past. Your father has gone to great pains to protect me—and you—from Scaddono."

"I'm sorry," I said.

"What for?"

"That you loved each other so much, and you've had so little time together."

"More than you think. We've managed a month every year. We've sneaked weekends or a few days when I could meet him somewhere, sometimes right under your nose. Our 'University sponsor' was a good companion all those years at lectures."

Tony was still barking orders, sending his men through the house again, out on the grounds with flashlights, taking the dogs in a further sweep of the estate.

"Get out and find 'em! I don't care what ya have to do! Find 'em! And get this mess out of here," he yelled, kicking the lifeless body at his feet.

They were off again. I settled back feeling contented. So many answers after all these years! Satisfying answers.

I had one problem . . . what to do about Bart and the wedding.

As I relaxed, a heavy weariness overpowered me. Adrenalin stopped flowing. Tomorrow's terror was over the horizon, and my body said it was time to stop. Mom looked at me.

"Snuggle by Bart and get a couple of hours' sleep. I had a long nap this afternoon and I'm wide awake."

Without objecting, I stretched out on the fur throw next to Bart, trying not to touch him, but his arm reached out and curled around me, pulling me close. I was too tired to worry about the emotions his nearness would evoke, but was surprised at how safe and secure I felt next to him.

"Are you awake?"

"No. I'm sound asleep."

"Do you put your arm around every body that comes close to you?"

"Natural reflex when a beautiful woman lays her body next to mine." His sleepy eyes were laughing. "You know I've never slept with another woman in my life."

"I wish I could believe that!" I was beyond even Kip bothering me now. I nestled in Bart's arms and fell into an exhausted but contented sleep. Had I known what awaited us tomorrow, I couldn't have closed my eyes.

Chapter Twenty-Three

Hours later I woke to the soft murmur of voices, alone on the fur throw. Bart and Dad were watching the latest developments with Tony, who'd apparently been up all night. I shut my eyes, not wanting anyone to know I was awake yet.

Shifting quietly, I observed Bart's animated expressions as he and Dad discussed obstacles in vanquishing Tony and Scaddono. As I watched these two men in my life, I was amazed at the differences in us. They thrived on danger and excitement. I didn't know how much sleep they'd had last night, probably not a great deal, but their eyes were alert, and they were eager with enthusiasm. Was that unique to the species? No. All men weren't like that.

I pictured several men I'd dated. Stan only looked like that when he was explaining mathematics to some neophyte. Mark came alive over horses, Richard's turn-on was boats, and Stuart's was his latest profit on the stock market. Milton? I wasn't sure what, if anything, would excite him. He was composed, unemotional, sedate about every aspect of his life. All of them would have shied away from putting their lives on the line day after day.

Watching these two, I knew they were a different breed,

not only craving action, but willing to lay down their lives for what they believed.

Even with the volume on the monitor turned low, I could hear Tony yelling. "Find Bart and you'll find the women! He's here somewhere—probably in a secret room!"

"Tony," Nate began, "it's morning. Why don't ya let the men get some shut-eye. We can't go all night and all day, too."

Tony's fury was feeding, energizing him. He needed nothing more, but no one else felt his passion for the chase. They were tired, and they didn't like the abuse he heaped on them.

I didn't move, reluctant to begin this day for what it could bring. *I felt like the sacrificial lamb, being led to the slaughter.*

I looked at Mom, peacefully sleeping across from me. How many nights had terror of Antonio Scaddono driven away peaceful rest? If, by going through with this outrageous plan, I could assure Mom of peaceful nights free from fear of Antonio, didn't I owe her that much? *I had to do it.*

Today's my wedding day. And where am I? Certainly not where I'd imagined. I'd pictured a leisurely brunch with our families at an elegant restaurant.

I sat up straight. *Maybe Bart could send Tony on a wild goose chase somewhere. Why should I let him spoil my wedding day, such as it was?*

Bart glanced over his shoulder when he heard my movement. "Oh, oh! I recognize that look!"

Dad turned around. "What is 'that look'?"

"That's her 'I'm determined' look."

Dad laughed. It was contagious. I laughed, too. That woke Mom.

"It's nice to wake up to the happy sound of my family. What have I missed?"

"What are you so determined to do?" Bart asked me.

"This is my wedding day. I've always dreamed of a lovely brunch with silver, crystal, tea roses and our families gathered around us. Either we're going into town to eat, or we'll get rid of Tony and goons and we'll have our wedding breakfast catered. Would you like to take me to El Encanto, or shall we have them deliver?"

I didn't think I'd asked for anything impossible but from the stunned looks on their faces, apparently they did. It was Mom's turn to laugh. Bart and Dad just looked at each other.

"I don't see that it's insurmountable," I insisted. "Every bride should have a special wish on her wedding day. You did tell Tony you need a happy bride. Which is it? In town or here?"

Dad actually snorted! "I can't believe you'd even think of such an impossibility!"

"What's impossible about it?" I asked.

"Your mother can't show her face until the wedding when we won't have problems protecting her."

"Get rid of Tony," I said simply.

Bart was thinking. "Maybe it's not so farfetched, if we can keep Tony on the ship long enough. I could send his hired friends on a treasure hunt to the ship for the kids and jewels."

Dad mulled it over for a few minutes. "Maybe it's worth a try. It would get them out of our hair for a while. All right!" He pointed a finger at me. "Don't you do a thing until we get it worked out downstairs and determine that they're out of the way."

I smiled. "Yes, sir!"

Dad turned to Bart. "What time did Tony say Scaddono was arriving?"

"Not till the critical hour—5:00."

Bart checked the monitors to make sure no one was near the front foyer, then he left, following Mom's suggestion that he use the passage into the foyer.

"The coast is clear," Dad reported in Bart's wrist radio. "The outside guard is by the corner of the house." Bart slipped quietly into the foyer, opened and closed the front door loudly as though he had just come in from outside, and yelled "Yo, Tony? Anybody here?"

On the screen we watched Tony's reaction to Bart's voice. He propelled off the sofa and into the foyer like a well-aimed bottle rocket.

"Bart!" he bellowed.

"There you are, Tony! What's going on? Anybody got breakfast ready?"

From adjoining rooms, the straggly-looking group of men gathered around Tony. Just what Bart wanted.

"Did you find the kids yet? And the jewels?"

Tony's dark scowl deepened. Bart was baiting him and he knew it.

"Do you suppose Sam hid the kids back on ship with the jewels?"

While Tony sputtered trying to get a word in, Bart fed the crew surrounding Tony.

"I haven't seen Sam lately. I'll bet he's on the ship with the kids and he intends to keep the jewels for himself."

By this time the curiosity of the crew won over their fear of Tony.

"Tell me about the jewels," one said eagerly.

"A whole bag full of diamonds, rubies, emeralds, sapphires—unset stones the size of my thumb that are worth several million." Then Bart stopped. "Tony! You've got some new help! Hi, guys. I'm Bart."

He made a great show of shaking hands with several of the closer crew. "Do they get a share of the profits, too? That'll sure diminish our cut, splitting it so many ways. Did you say you'd searched the ship?"

Then finally Bart stopped and looked directly at Tony. The hate on Tony's face was so intense I could almost feel it.

Be careful, Bart! Don't push him too far!

The murmuring of the men grew.

"What's keeping us? Let's go look now!"

"Come on, Tony, what're ya waitin' for? They're not here and we haven't searched the ship."

Tony was beat and he knew it. "Okay. We'll search the ship. But I want a couple of you to stay here."

"Not me!" a chorus of protests rang out.

"It's okay, Tony. I'll be here. I've got to keep an eye on my bride," Bart said.

Tony was so mad I thought he'd erupt! Bart must have sensed he'd pushed Tony too far because he backed off. Nate knew that Tony's fuse was at its end and he steered Tony toward the door.

"I think that's a good idea, boss. We haven't searched there. There's a million places Sam could hide those kids. Let's go look."

The greedy clamor through the door drowned out everything else. I was thrilled. That should keep them busy for several hours. Time enough for a luxurious soak in the tub, a leisurely brunch and whatever else I needed to do to get ready for my wedding day. *I wish I didn't get a sick feeling every time I thought about it.*

I ordered brunch for six to be delivered at 10:00 a.m. It was amazing to see what accommodations I was granted when Margo's name was mentioned.

We watched happily on the monitors as they left. Bart

walked them out, making sure everyone got on the boat, including the guard Tony had left at the front door.

"I'll tell you what I'm going to do right now," I announced. "I'm going to pamper myself with a hot tub full of bubbles."

"Stay here in the house where we can keep a closer eye on things and make sure you're not disturbed," Dad suggested. "If Tony does come back, we can get you hidden fast."

It was terrifying to realize the next few hours held life or death for so many. If Antonio Scaddono accomplished his plan, our lives were over—all six of us. And how many more? Another bloodbath, like so many others he'd orchestrated.

I took the guest room next to Margo's bedroom . . . Mom's bedroom. Bubbles multiplied and exploded as I poured in more bubble bath and sank to my chin in the luxuriant froth. I tried to relax, to enjoy the momentary lull from Tony's threatening presence.

We have to win. Please bless us in this, I prayed, remembering Bart's simple but fervent prayer on the Azores. I longed to know what had happened to Bart in Tibet and about his newfound faith. When this was over. Then there would be time to hear—if we won.

I explored Mom's closet for something to wear, choosing a tailored white silk blouse and navy wool crepe skirt. They fit.

In Margo's jewel boxes, I found a pair of emerald cufflinks and slipped them in the French cuffs, a perfect complement to my emerald engagement ring. Then a realization struck me. These were Mom's jewels! All of this was Mom's!

I sank weak-kneed onto the plum velvet vanity stool. Gazing at the opulence around me, I had difficulty comprehending this was Mom's life once.

A loud banging on the door interrupted my musing.

"Are you going to stay in there forever?"

"Come in."

It was Bart, clean-shaven, in clean clothes, looking like a new man.

"Wow! Look at you! Have you been to your apartment?"

"No. I figured the folks were probably back from their vacation and called them. They can't stay away very long."

Suddenly I felt selfish. "I didn't even think about your folks. They'd be so hurt if they missed your wedding."

"They're here now. I had them bring some clothes from my apartment and their Sunday best. Told them I'd have a special treat for them."

"Is it safe?"

"As safe for them as for you and your folks." He put his arms around my waist.

"It's all right, Princess. We can do this. By the way, thanks for trusting me. I promise . . ."

I searched his face as he paused, then put my finger on his lips.

"Don't promise anything that you can't deliver. I can't handle any more disappointments."

Disappointments. How many would there be after this mock wedding I'd agreed to for Mom's sake? First, Bart's parents would be devastated to find it was a sham. And Mom and Dad. And me.

"I promise you won't be sorry."

I leaned my head against his chest with resignation. "I want to believe that." Bart's arms slid comfortably around me.

"I promise," he whispered in my hair. I needed that reassurance more than he could possibly guess. *Why couldn't I believe it?* Suddenly I looked at the time.

"Good grief! It's nearly ten o'clock! I've got to hurry! Breakfast will be here any minute."

I flew into action.

"Make sure everybody's ready and watch for the caterer. I've got to set the table. Make sure Tony doesn't show up to ruin everything!"

"Yes, Your Highness. Your wish is my command." Bart laughed after me as I skipped down the stairs. I was almost light-headed with temporary relief from the oppressive danger of the past several days. *Now, if only I had confidence in this marriage plan . . . .*

Throwing wide the doors on Margo's linen closet, I chose a Battenburg lace cloth. Bart's mom came in with a delighted smile.

"Allison, I'm so happy!" She gave me a quick hug.

"Alma! I'm glad you got back in time. It wouldn't have been complete without you."

"I hoped you and Bart would find each other again." She sincerely meant it. "Can I help?"

"Please! We need silver and napkins. Here's the china."

The front door flew open and Sunny and Boomer burst through. "It's here!" Bart trooped in behind them with his dad in tow.

"Hi, Jim," I welcomed Bart's dad.

"Bart told me your good news. Welcome to the family."

"Thank you. I've always felt like part of the family." *That was true, but everything I was doing now was a lie that would break their hearts when they discovered the truth.*

"You have been. This just makes it official." Jim grinned. "We worried Bart would wait too long and let some fancy New York dude snatch you away. Glad that didn't happen."

Mom and Dad came down the stairs arm in arm, looking refreshed.

The delivery boy from El Encanto made his way in under a tray laden with beautifully prepared food. I led him to the dining room, then turned to see a second courier with another tray.

The frightful circumstances of Tony's presence were temporarily pushed aside while we enjoyed this peaceful interlude. As I directed everyone to their places, I felt a tug at my skirt and looked into the saddest eyes I'd ever seen. I lifted Sunny into my arms.

"What's the matter, sweetheart?"

She buried her face in my shoulder and clung tightly to my neck.

"Are you okay?"

"She's homesick, Miss Allison."

Bart whispered something in her ear that electrified her. She raised her head, her eyes filled with delight.

"Will you let me in on your secret?"

Bart grinned. "Shall we keep it our secret, Sunny?"

She giggled. "Okay." With a hug, she said, "You'll see."

I sat with Sunny on one side and Bart on the other. Even Tony's shadow hanging over us failed to dim this bright moment when I was finally surrounded by those I loved most. *Tony!*

"Who's watching the boat? What if Tony comes back?"

"Our guardian angels are in place. They'll let us know." Dad said.

Jim raised his goblet of apricot nectar. "Is it proper to toast with juice at breakfast? A toast to Margo's homecoming," he smiled fondly at Mom, "to Jack's resurrection, and to Bart and Allison—a long and happy life!"

"Hear! Hear!" Dad exclaimed.

"I'd like to propose a toast," Bart said. He stood and raised his goblet. "To Margaret, who conceived the idea, to the engineering genius of my father and Jack, who designed and built the secret passageways that have made our survival thus far possible, and the courage and skill which will bring this day to a happy and successful close."

"Hear. Hear." Mom said softly with an ever so slight quiver in her voice. *Were our thoughts similar? This day must ultimately bring freedom—or death. How was it possible to feel so frightened and so calm at the same time?*

Chapter Twenty-Four

Our blissful breakfast bubble was abruptly shattered by the crackle of Dad's wrist radio.

"Heads up, Jack. The boat's coming back."

"How long have we got?" Dad questioned into his radio.

"Twenty minutes at the most."

Dad barked orders like a company commander.

"Jim, take Boomer and Sunny back to the secret room. You three get rid of this," waving toward the table, "then get back upstairs. Bart, come with me."

Everyone hastened to their appointed tasks, then fled to the safety of the secret room. We watched on the monitor as Tony and four of the biggest, ugliest gunmen I'd ever seen stormed through the front door into the grand foyer.

"Bart!" he roared. "Bart!" Tony stood with his hands on his hips and feet apart in a James Cagney gangster pose. We watched on the monitor as Bart sauntered slowly down the spiral staircase.

"You called, Tony?"

"Whose car's that?"

"My folks. You didn't think I'd get married without my parents here."

Tony looked surprised.

"Tony! We have to make it look real. It's got to be a nice, neat little package, all tied up with family and a real preacher. Scaddono wants no questions as to the legality of this."

Tony snorted. "I need that paper. Scaddono will be here in a couple of hours, and he'll want it first thing."

"We've been busy. I haven't had time to get her to sign it, but I'll get it to you."

"You're damn right you'll get it to me—right now!"

"I'll go. . . ."

"No! You won't go! I want her here in front of me. NOW!"

Bart knew we were watching every move and nuance on the monitors, but for effect he called loudly up the stairs. "Allison, can you come down for a minute, please?"

I looked at Dad.

"It's all right, Bunny. We'll be at the top of the stairs if he tries anything."

He took Mom's gun from her and handed it to Jim. "You've just been recruited. Remember how to use this?"

Jim smiled. "Just like riding a bicycle. Once you learn, you never forget."

We slipped down the stairs and exited the secret passage into Margo's closet. I left Dad and Jim just out of sight on either side of the spiral staircase while I descended. Bart came up a couple of steps and squeezed my hand reassuringly.

"You remember Tony, but I don't think you've met Larry, Curly, Moe, and Twinkle Toes," Bart said facetiously, pointing to each of the huge gunmen who dwarfed Tony.

"Tony wants to make sure everything's tied up nice and legal. He'd like us to sign a pre-nuptial agreement. In case anything happens to me, everything I have is yours and if anything happens to you, everything you have is mine. Would you mind, sweetheart?"

"Is that necessary under California law?"

Tony grinned maliciously. "Humor me."

I found some paper and came back into the dining room. Bart tried to position himself between us but Tony was faster this time.

"Back off, Tony!" Bart warned.

Tony hissed, "No! You back off!" He grabbed a handful of my hair, jerking my head violently backward, and jabbed the gun into my neck. "You're not in charge here. I am! Make no mistake! I want the paper, the jewels, the kids, and my men, and I want 'em now!"

He tugged harder on my hair, yanking my head further. "You took 'em, didn't ya'? You've got the kids. The jewels, too?"

I bit my lip to keep from crying out. I only had one gun pointed at me. Bart had four. I hoped he had the good sense not to try any heroics with these odds.

"I'll have a hard time writing with my head in this position. Would you mind letting go?" I said, as calmly as I could. I didn't feel calm. I was terrified. My heart was racing. My mouth was dry. I could hardly talk. I hoped Tony didn't notice the quiver in my voice as I asked, "Would you like to dictate it?"

Tony relaxed his hold on me a bit and let my head come forward, though he didn't let go. His fingers still gripped my hair so tight it caused a headache.

"Sit down!" he commanded, shoving me into the chair.

"Tony, please let go. I'm doing what you asked. It's impossible to write with my head back. Please, remove the gun from my neck. You're cutting off my circulation. I'm going to faint." He let go of my hair and shoved my head forward with such force I thought my neck would snap.

Backing away slightly and motioning to one of the goons holding a gun on Bart, he asked, "You! Sampson! Think you could convince Bart to be more humble and cooperative?"

Sampson hit Bart full in the stomach with such force it lifted him off his feet and slammed him into the wall. Bart slumped to the floor, doubled over with pain.

"Like that, boss?" Sampson grinned maliciously. He picked Bart up and dumped him in the chair next to mine.

I dutifully copied what Tony dictated, then Bart added his bit on the bottom. Tony seized the paper triumphantly and waved it over us.

"Finally! I'll have my retribution!"

"Retribution for what?" I asked innocently. "How does that paper help you? I thought that was for Antonio Scaddono."

Tony's smirk turned into a sneer. He raised his hand to strike me but in a move that caught everyone off guard, Bart grabbed Tony's raised wrist with a steely grip and his gun hand with another, shoving the gun deep into Tony's paunch.

"Call off your goons, Tony. Tell them to drop their guns and find the door."

Torn between ordering the four big guys to take Bart and the fear that the gun jabbing painfully in his stomach would go off, either accidentally or on purpose, Tony searched wild-eyed for an opening. Nobody moved. Finally, four guns hit the floor and their former handlers backed slowly away.

"Don't misjudge me, Tony," Bart said quietly, but with a savage intensity I'd never heard in his voice. "You haven't got enough men to protect you if you hurt Allison. Get out of my sight before I kill you."

He motioned the four into the foyer, forcing Tony in the same direction, slowly, carefully, step by step backwards to join them, the gun still pressed deep in Tony's stomach, Bart's other hand grasping Tony's wrist.

The four stood with hands hanging limply by their sides, confused. Nobody ordered Tony around. They weren't sure who to obey. Taking advantage of their bewilderment, Bart ushered them out. Tony stormed ahead of his men, muttering obscenities all the way.

"Get your goons out of sight, Tony. All of them. The press will be here any time to record pretty faces, not your ugly ones!"

As Bart slammed the door behind Tony, I fell limply into his arms, relieved to have the repulsive rat out of my sight.

Bart winced as I hugged him.

"Are you okay?"

Bart felt the battered area.

"I don't think he broke anything, but it knocked the wind out of me."

Dad and Jim came cautiously down the marble staircase. They had heard every word.

"Sorry, Alli. That was a bad call. We'll make sure they don't get close to any of you the rest of the day. Are you okay?" Dad looked at me carefully, then pulled me close. "I'd never forgive myself if anything happened to you!" he whispered softly.

Jim checked to see if Tony and company actually were leaving. We watched from the window as they spread out along the top of the cliff looking for the kids, then headed down the path to the beach.

As the group descended the trail, a car entered the circular drive. Madame Shuang, elegantly attired in an emerald silk suit, approached the house carrying a bag. My dress filled the back of the car. Beaming broadly, Bart threw the door open wide.

"Good morning, Madame Shuang. You look radiant." He bowed formally and ushered her into the sitting room.

"Will you wait here?"

"Margaret," he said into his wrist radio. "Send Boomer and Sunny down."

There was no need. They'd seen her arrival on the monitor and burst into the foyer like two genies out of a bottle, nearly overpowering the tiny Madame Shuang.

Bart and Dad couldn't have been more satisfied with the scene before us as the two royal children were greeted lovingly and with much relief at their safety. Madame Shuang checked them over from head to toe as if she expected to find them bruised and battered.

"Okay. Who's going to tell me the real story here?" I demanded.

Bart laughed. "Her son did make your wedding dress. I fudged on her introduction. Madame Shuang's been the children's governess since they were born. King Bhumibol sent her to bring them home."

Dad added, "She belongs to the royal family—she's a cousin or something."

They chattered excitedly in their native language until Madame Shuang put her finger to her lips. Immediately they fell silent.

"English, please," she said softly. "It is not good manners to speak when others do not understand."

While Sunny and Boomer recounted their adventures, I watched Madame Shuang's reactions, worried she'd be upset about their treatment. I read only satisfaction that they had handled themselves so well.

"I was afraid she'd be unhappy they spent days and nights

in a tree and freezing under the waterfall," I said to Dad.

"Actually, the old king wants them to know what it's like to live in the real world, to become independent and self-reliant, and not to depend on palace guards to protect them. This has probably been not only fun and exciting for them, but a marvelous learning experience, too."

"Do you have any more surprises for me?"

"No, but now would be a good time to retrieve the royal jewels and return them to Madame Shuang."

I led them into the library and up the circular staircase.

"They're here?" Dad questioned.

"Right here in plain sight. Can you see them?"

"No."

I leaned over the railing, reached out to the chandelier and peeled the cellophane tape free from a crystal tear-drop. Dangling from the clear tape was a huge diamond.

"I remember that movie!" laughed Bart. "It was a Hitchcock film."

"Ingenious, Allison!" exclaimed Dad.

I peeled off all the diamonds, retrieved the velvet pouch from under the music books where it was stashed, and handed them to Dad.

"What about the colored stones?"

"They're in Margo's rainbow-colored chandelier." We trooped through the well-traveled secret passage between library and bedroom. I leaned over the balcony to the chandelier and gathered the colored stones.

"It's a good thing nobody thought to look up," Bart laughed. "These stones don't match the chandelier at all."

"Men don't usually notice things like that, and it was the best I could do in the dark."

Boomer was delighted. "I can't wait to tell my father and grandfather where you hid the jewels! You are a very smart lady!"

Sunny tugged on my skirt. I picked her up and held her. She grabbed my neck in her familiar bear hug.

"I'll miss you when you go back home, Sunny."

"I'll miss you, Miss Allison, but . . ."

"I know, sweetheart. You miss your mom. You should be home with her."

"Will you come to see me?"

"I'd love to."

"Maybe we ought to send the honeymooning couple to Bangkok as an escort for Madame Shuang and the children."

I turned with excitement to see if Dad was serious, but he was ceremoniously placing the black velvet bag into Madame Shuang's hands. It was a relief to transfer the precious gems to Madame Shuang, along with full care of Boomer and Sunny.

"You and I have a secret mission to perform," Bart announced mysteriously, motioning for me to follow him.

Chapter Twenty-Five

As Bart pulled me through the French doors into the serenity of the formal gardens, we passed through portals from a world of danger and violence into one of peace and beauty. We were assailed by the sweet fragrance of blossoms and the visual splendor of the gardens. A peacock fanned his kaleidoscopic tail, flaunting his magnificent beauty.

We paused, entranced, savoring the enchantment of the moment, the unexpected tranquility. I leaned against Bart. He felt good next to me. The dreaded fear, pain, and nausea that usually accompanied thoughts of marriage—or Bart—were absent!

Another realization swept me—how much I loved this gentle man who surprised me with his inner strength, his ability to lighten a heavy moment with humor, his sharp mind, and his concern for me. He tilted my chin up and brushed a soft kiss across the tip of my nose and my lips.

My heart snapped a picture of this moment and locked it away deep inside. Now I knew what Mom meant when she said, "Savor the sweet moments and remember them when you're apart." This would be a memory I could pull up to relive later when I was alone.

A pang of panic stabbed me. *I don't want to be alone after this. I want . . .*

"Bart," I hesitated. I spoke over a dozen different languages, but I couldn't find the right words in my own. "I need to know . . . what happens after the wedding?"

"The Feds will close in and take everyone into custody."

"No . . . after everything is settled down."

Bart's blue eyes sparkled. "We'll go on our honeymoon and spend the rest of our lives learning to live happily ever after."

His answer caught me off guard. Whatever I expected, that wasn't it!

"You're serious?" I gasped.

The laughter left his eyes. He became serious. The quiet tone in his voice, when he finally spoke, was edgy, cautious. "What did you want to happen when you agreed to this?"

"I agreed to pretend. This is real, with real vows of commitment. I have to know what you're planning afterward. An annulment?"

"You're the only one pretending, Allison. I never have been. I asked you to pretend, hoping you'd come to understand how I really felt about you. If you don't know, if you want an annulment, I won't fight it. But that's not what I want. Do you know what I want? I want you by my side for the rest of my life and beyond. I want you to have our children. I want our family to be together forever."

"Bart, I can't imagine you marrying a pesky little sister and having it be anything more than a sham. Though you vow undying, eternal love, your picture of me as a little sister shines through too often to make it work." *I want to believe him. Why can't I?*

We resumed our walk silently through the garden. *Hadn't they planned beyond the wedding and the capture of Tony and*

Scaddono? That didn't seem logical. They were supposed to be strategists, covering every angle. *Had they forgotten me?*

It felt like an armed truce as we wound our way through green maze splashed by forsythia, wisteria, and the rainbow of roses Mom said Margo loved so much. It made so much sense. Why hadn't I seen it before?

"I feel stupid, not connecting Mom and Margo."

"You had no reason to. It took Scaddono twenty years to associate them."

"How did he find out?"

"After searching for Margo in the Far East, he started from this end, planting a clerk in the bank who went through all the estate accounts. The clerk eventually found Margo's signature and your mom's signature on something. He saw similarities and a handwriting expert matched them up."

The golf cart Jim used to traverse the grounds was parked at the cabanas, loaded with Margo's silver candelabrum.

"Somebody had to take care of things while you soaked the morning away." Bart laughed at my surprise.

A bright, spring sun warmed us as we rode down the hill and across the beautifully kept lawn. We arranged the candelabrum in and around the rock formation I'd named the sacrificial altar. *How appropriate!*

"It'll take longer to light the candles than perform the ceremony."

"We'll assign that to the folks, if the wind isn't too high."

I watched him across the altar, arranging the candelabrum.

Why can't he see me as I am? If he hadn't stayed away those last five years, he might not think of me as a pesky little sister. This wedding might . . .

"Bart, why did Tony say *he* was finally going to have *his* retribution?"

Bart stood up and looked at me.

"That's what he said, wasn't it?"

"I was so rattled at the time, it didn't register. You don't suppose . . ."

"I think, my pretty little princess, that you might just have discovered a component we didn't even know was missing."

We jumped in the cart and raced back to the communication center. Mom and Dad were there. We pulled the files and Bart and Dad compared the file photos of Antonio Scaddono and Tony.

"Suppose you take forty pounds off Scaddono, dye the hair and shave the beard. What do you have?"

"Tony!" Mom gasped. Dad hurried to informed the agents that were staked out but returned with the news that Tony had disappeared in a white Mercedes.

"Now what do we do?" I asked.

"Go on with the plan," Dad replied. "Scaddono was supposed to show for the wedding. We'll hope he does. But now we know who we're really looking for. Bunny, you'd better get dressed."

Everyone looked at me. *Chin up, lady. Let's see how good an actress you really are!*

"Let's do it!" I said cheerfully, feeling anything but. Everyone dispersed to get ready for the wedding—for the trap. *Who would be caught?*

"Are you Margaret, the mother of the bride, or is this the formal unveiling of Margo?"

"If Margo comes back, she'll never be free from the paparazzi. If she doesn't, there's no case against Scaddono. Neither Margo nor Margaret will be free until he's out of the way. For now, I'm the mother of the bride."

She pulled a cream linen suit from the closet and we began dressing for this strange wedding.

Some time later, Dad knocked at the door.

"Are you two coming out? You've been closeted for over two hours! The wedding party's waiting for the bride and her beautiful mother."

Mom fluffed my veil one last time and stepped back to survey me.

"Without a doubt, the most beautiful bride I've ever seen!" Behind the bright smile, a sadness shrouded her happiness.

"Have you decided?" I knew the question that was on her mind.

She shook her head and opened the door.

"How did I get the two most gorgeous creatures in the world?" Dad exclaimed.

"Just lucky," I laughed. Then, quietly I asked, "Is Tony back?"

"No, not yet."

He offered us each an arm and we descended the marble spiral staircase.

As we approached the last corner, Dad gave me a gentle shove. "Bunny, this is your day. Go for it!"

My day! Some day! Where's Tony? What's he planning?

"Smile!" Mom whispered.

I did. In my best bride fashion, I floated down the white marble staircase. Cory Black's photographer was filming. Jim and Alma waited at the bottom of the stairs.

I recognized faces from high school days—good friends who'd married and settled nearby, Mom's colleagues from the college, and two of Mom's close friends. There were faces I'd never seen before. *Who are these strangers at my wedding? Tony's men or government agents?*

Jim stepped forward as I reached the bottom of the staircase.

"Your chariot awaits. May I escort you?"

"Thank you, I'd be honored."

I couldn't believe what waited in the driveway. A train of golf carts, gaily decorated with white satin streamers and bows, was ready to transport the wedding party across the lawns to the altar. Jim and Alma had been busy.

Bishop O'Hare stepped forward in a business suit. I was ashamed that he read my expression so clearly. He explained, "In The Church of Jesus Christ of Latter-day Saints, we don't wear the collar and robes you associate with clergy. We conduct the business of the church in street clothes. Disappointed?"

"No," I laughed. "As long as you have authority, I don't care what you wear . . . almost!" *But if he didn't have authority, then I wouldn't have to be married.*

Jim and Alma arranged my dress while the guests piled into the waiting carts. Bishop O'Hare drove my cart, with Mom, Dad, Jim, and Alma following. The third cart carried Madam Shuang and a delighted Boomer and Sunny.

"Are you worried?"

I looked at Bishop O'Hare. "About what?"

"Scaddono and his plans for your family."

"Bart told you?"

"Allison, in our church, we have a lay ministry. Everyone holds full-time jobs, in addition to our church responsibilities. Bart came to me for two reasons. I assumed he'd told you. I'm with the FBI."

I was stunned. "And the other?"

Now he looked at me. "He has told you about his conversion, hasn't he? That was the second reason—to arrange for a series of lessons, or 'discussions,' prior to his baptism."

Fortunately, there wasn't time to reply. What could I have said? Each new staggering revelation had no time to be absorbed before I was hit with another. Bart zoomed across the lawns, coattails flying, parked his cart behind a huge boulder, and waited at the altar for us.

Our guests parked their carts in a large semi-circle several yards back, *like the circling of the wagons against the Indians?*

Mom and Dad were at my side. Jim and Alma stood with Bart. Bishop O'Hare took his place behind the natural altar.

Roses had been delivered and lit candles shone in the candelabrum. It was breathtaking. The waterfall warbled in the background. Where was Tony?

As twilight descended, we knelt at the altar. *If only this were authentic. If Bart loved me . . . if this wasn't simply a plan to free Mom from the threat she'd been under for twenty years . . . if, if, if!*

Bishop O'Hare began. "We are gathered here . . ." The flash of the camera was dim compared to the light in Bart's eyes. He was putting his heart into this. *I wish I could. I wish this wasn't a charade we'll have to undo later. I wish I didn't have lead in the pit of my stomach.* I don't remember a thing the bishop said. His pleasant, lyrical voice droned on and on. I became lost in the blue mist of Bart's eyes. Even the threat of Tony faded away.

I was grateful for the satin pad someone had put down for us to kneel on. Suddenly, the dreaded question pierced the mist, snapping me back to reality. "Will you, Melanie Allison Alexander, take Bartholomew James Allan to be your lawfully wedded husband . . ."

I didn't hear any more, though Bishop O'Hare's lips were still moving. Panic obliterated everything but Bart clinging tightly to my hands, preventing me from running away. Then I was aware of anticipatory silence. I looked at the bishop, then at Bart. Both waited for my answer. I couldn't stand the look of anxiety in Bart's eyes.

I dropped my head and whispered "I do . . . yes." I couldn't even remember what I was supposed to say!

Bart's relief was obvious. He had no trouble with his answer. I was having trouble breathing.

I finally heard, "I now pronounce you, Bartholomew James Allan and Melanie Allison Alexander, husband and wife. Do you have rings to exchange?" I didn't.

Boomer presented a platinum wedding band on a white velvet cushion. I slipped the emerald from my finger and Bart replaced it with the wedding band, then restored the emerald. He held my hand, brought it to his lips and kissed my palm, his eyes never leaving mine. *Why can't this be for real?* my heart cried!

Sunny offered the contents of her miniature velvet cushion with a dimpled smile.

Mom whispered, "I don't think it's bad luck for the groom to provide his own wedding band when it's inscribed like this." Inside the matching band was engraved, "Property of the Princess."

I looked at Bart. *This was carrying things too far.*

"Do you believe me now?" Bart whispered. "I love you. I've always loved you. I want you as my wife—forever—not just till death do us part. Allison, if you'll believe me, I can give you not only forever, but everything we ever dreamed of, everything we talked about all those years ago."

I looked at him for a long minute, forgetting everyone waiting and watching, forgetting Tony and the danger we were in now that these vows were solemnized. *Does he mean it? Can I believe him?* I looked at the ring with its inscription. *Yes. Yes!*

"As long as you remember that when some ravishing foreign agent is trying to seduce you," I whispered, slipping the ring on Bart's finger.

"You may now kiss the bride."

Bart stood up, lifting me to my feet, and kissed away every doubt.

Suddenly an explosion rocked the estate. The bishop lunged at us and we hit the ground. Bart's golf cart, parked behind the rocks, blew into a million pieces. A second explosion shattered the air.

The guests flattened in the grass. One after another the carts exploded, showering shrapnel over the area.

"Bishop, your long ceremony saved our lives," Bart said. "Those bombs must have been set to go off as we returned to the house. Tony wasn't taking chances we'd trade carts. He would've wiped out the whole party."

"Bunny, are you all right?"

"Yes, Dad, but my dress is probably ruined!"

"I can't believe you'd think of it at a time like this!"

"Bishop, look after her. We've got some bad guys to catch." Bart blew me a kiss and he and Dad raced across the lawn.

A couple of gray-suited FBI men materialized and hurried us to safety behind the rocks. The bishop shepherded the guests to shelter behind other rocks while Cory Black's photographer recorded everything. This would headline the late news!

I watched Dad and Bart's progress up the hill, and half a dozen gray suits converging on the house ahead of them.

Cory dashed toward us with her camera-toting bear. I had an idea.

"What's going on?" She shoved a microphone in my face while the video camera blinked its recording light.

I took a deep breath and began. "Here's your story. When

Margo was performing for the troops in Vietnam years ago, she witnessed the massacre of an important political family by Antonio Scaddono. She could identify him so he tried to eliminate her. To survive, Margo disappeared, assuming a new identity. Scaddono became a drug czar and wanted to broaden his operations to the States."

I pulled Mom close. "Margo's sister agreed to impersonate her to flush out Scaddono so authorities could apprehend him before he got organized here. He wasn't sure which cart Margo would be in, so Tony blew them all up. This wonderful, long-winded bishop saved our lives."

"But what about Margo?" Cory questioned, pointing the microphone at Mom.

"Happy with her life the way it is. Margo's gone forever."

Suddenly a barrage of shots echoed from the house.

"I wish I'd left my wrist radio on," Mom whispered.

Dad! Are you all right? No answer. I knew the fear Mom had lived with for twenty years. *Dad! Answer me!*

Chapter Twenty-Six

My answer was a thunderous explosion. As we watched, horrified, the entire back of the house disappeared in a gigantic fireball. Another explosion rocked the grounds, then a third. The entire back of Margo's . . . Mom's beautiful home erupted!

We dashed for the house. I removed my shoes, discarded my veil and train, and gathered my dress above my knees so I could run unhindered.

"Call the fire department," I yelled to the agent behind me.

"I did." He passed us on the run, radio in hand.

Fire was visible in the gathering dusk, flames licking at the exposed beams, blazing into the air.

Dad, are you all right? What's happening? I telepathed, racing across the lawn and up the hill.

Flames flared bright orange against the darkening sky, leaping, dancing, devouring everything they touched.

Where are you? Where's Bart? My head ached from concentrating. My heart and lungs bursting from the steep uphill run.

Did no answer mean he was unconscious—or worse? I

ejected the thought forcibly from my mind. Where were they when the first explosion occurred? If their timing was wrong, they'd have been in the middle of it. If they were fast enough to be beyond the first explosion, surely the second or third would have caught them . . . they were in harm's way no matter what.

I glimpsed shadowy figures here and there through the flames and tried to reach Dad.

Are you okay? Answer me! Still nothing.

We were winded as we reached the house. Heat and flames were too intense in back, so Mom and I raced toward the front, dodging chairs, beds, and pieces of walls and doors blown free in the explosion. Stopping only long enough to put my shoes back on, I fled past these broken, twisted objects, trying not to think what such an explosion would do to a man's body.

Miraculously, the front of the house seemed intact. The windows were shattered, but the walls were still standing. The fire hadn't reached here. Mom was at my heels.

"Search the house! I'm going to the garden."

I flew through the music room, calling, searching, through the ballroom and the library, shouting anxiously for Bart—for Dad—telepathing the same frantic message. *Where are you? Are you okay?* Nothing.

A door blocked the hall beyond. I didn't remember a door there. Turning back, I raced down the hall to the other wing. Empty.

Dad! Please hear me! Where are you? Where's Bart?

Had Mom found something in the garden? As I stepped through the French doors, smoke burned my eyes, my lungs. I staggered back and bumped into something solid . . . and human.

A strong arm circled my waist, pinning my arms to my

sides while a hand covered my mouth and nose, cutting off all air.

"If it isn't the lovely bride," a gravelly voice jeered.

Not human! Tony!

Tony's got me! I telepathed, beside myself with fear. *Wherever you are, hear me! Help me!*

My fear of Tony was consummate. I knew nothing would give him more pleasure than to get back at my parents by harming me in some diabolical way.

"You're gonna be my safe passage out of here."

Dad! I was desperate. *Tony's got me! Help me!* I could not let him take me. When he was through using me as a shield and a hostage, Tony would kill me.

He moved backward through the French doors into the upstairs foyer, carrying me with him. Wiggling and squirming, I fought to free myself, but he held me tighter. Suddenly I went limp, slumping against Tony with my full weight. It caught him off guard and he took the hand from my mouth to support my sagging body. I rammed my head backward as hard as I could when he bent, catching him full in the mouth, smashing his nose with the top of my head. Bellowing in pain, he grabbed his face to stem the bloody flow gushing from his nose and split lip.

I dropped out of his reach and flung myself into the smoke-filled darkness, stumbling down the curved staircase toward the garden.

"Bart!" I screamed. "Dad! Anybody! Tony's here!"

"Shut up, you witch!" Tony roared from somewhere above my head. Shots peppered the stairs behind me, followed by heavy footsteps.

I rolled over the balustrade as Tony lunged for me, landing in the soft dirt behind the rose bushes. *A wedding dress is a definite disadvantage, but I know the garden.* Darting through the narrow walkway under the stairs, I wriggled out the other side, avoiding the thorns tearing at my hair, my arms, my dress.

Tony cursed in the smoky shadows behind me. He'd found the walkway and was on my side of the stairs.

I'd seen agents hovering everywhere before the wedding and after the explosions. Where were they when I needed them?

The fire made eerie, dancing shapes of shrubs and bushes. I moved from shadow to shadow, away from Tony, but each movement took me closer to the inferno raging beyond the pool and into the glowing light.

Dad, if ever I needed you, it's now. I'm trapped between the fire and Tony. Help me!

I was out of hiding places. Crouching low behind the end of the maze, I looked frantically for my next cover. There was none. I could hear Tony right behind me.

My lungs and throat were burning from inhaling heavy smoke-filled air. The cough I'd stifled to keep Tony from finding me burst forth, and he followed it with a roar and an oath.

"Gotcha!" he shouted triumphantly and lunged to grab me. The rough hands I expected to feel never arrived. Out of the smoky night, a form hurtled through the air, smashing into Tony like a thunderbolt. I winced as the two men hit the ground with a bone-crunching thud and rolled and tussled through the flower beds.

I couldn't identify my benefactor even after they gained their footing. They were out of the firelight, in the shadowy maze, exchanging blows. Could I improve the odds for my rescuer?

Under the stairs, Jim stored lumber to repair the rose arbor. I retrieved a hefty piece and raced back to the battleground, ready to pounce when they emerged from the maze into the fire's glow.

A body burst through backwards and another immediately after with a gun in his hand. I couldn't tell who they were! The man on the ground jumped to his feet, heading back into the fray when he was stopped by a hate-filled gravelly command.

"Stop right there or you're a dead man!" Then a malicious laugh. "Don't matter. You're a dead man anyway. This'll give me the most pleasure I've ever had, Bart, getting rid of the biggest pain in the . . ."

Bart! I raised my weapon over my head, moving silently forward, keeping as much behind Tony as I could without brushing the shrubs. I couldn't chance him seeing me out of the corner of his eye, or hearing me. He'd simply shoot me first, and then Bart.

Bart saw me as I emerged from the shadows and took his cue. Dropping to one knee, he posed as a tired, bested man.

"I've got to hand it to you, Tony. You're a better man than I am. You're smarter, tougher . . ."

"Richer, and alive. Which you're not gonna be. You lied to me, Bart. You had them kids all the time, and the stones. But it don't matter. I don't need them, or you, or any of this."

He waved the gun in an arc just as I got within swinging distance, turning slightly as he did, and saw me move. I came down hard with the two-by-four as the gun exploded in my face. Bart hit the ground rolling. Tony turned as he fell, a stunned looked of pain and surprise on his face before he toppled into the grass and lay quiet.

"Bart!" I held my breath and flew across the ash-covered grass to where he lay.

"Bart!" He was still. Too still. I cradled his head, searching for bullet wounds or blood. I felt for a pulse and finally found it.

I was aware of movement behind me, voices, but my whole concentration was on this limp form in my arms. He stirred, opened his eyes, and felt his head.

"I know how you felt in the airplane when you hit your head. What kicked me?"

"I think a concrete gargoyle when you rolled. Are you okay?"

Bart struggled to stand and pulled me to my feet, holding me at arm's length. "You're a mess. After all the trouble I went to for that dress . . ."

"You're a pretty sorry sight yourself. Where's Dad? And Mom? What happened?"

"Probably around front. We'd come in by the cabanas when the north end of the house exploded, knocking us into the pool, along with half the patio furniture and cabanas. That saved our lives. The fireball that followed or the walls tumbling on us would have got us if we'd still been on the patio. Your dad took a nasty blow to the head, and I had to keep him afloat until someone could untangle us from the debris and drag us out."

Turning to the men behind us, he asked, "To which of you do I owe my life?"

"All of us, including Miss Alexander. Anastasia bit off more that she could chew this time. You're lucky we were here," one of the agents ragged him.

"You're right, Arneson," Bart rejoined. "Many thanks. Is he dead?"

"Quite, between the two-by-four to the head and the shot in the heart. Saves the government a bundle in legal fees, appeals, and incarceration."

"Cost Margo a pretty penny, though," another offered.

I gazed at the remains of the house, three quarters of it still blazing.

"Did you get the rest of his gang rounded up?" Bart asked.

"Yes, and we retrieved your captives. That was powerful stuff you administered. They're all complaining of migraine headaches," Agent Arneson said.

"They'll recover. Did you get Nate?"

"No. When did you see him last?"

Bart looked at me.

"Not since this morning when Tony shot that fellow."

"True. Has the Coast Guard taken the ship?" Bart asked.

"Yes, with a skeleton crew aboard. No Nate."

"That's too bad. He'll pick up where Tony left off. Get out an APB on him. Maybe we can catch him before he leaves the country."

"Right." Arneson took off. My immediate need was to find Mom and Dad.

Bart walked me up the stairs. We turned at the top to survey the tragic remains of the garden and the fires being smothered by fire hoses.

"Kind of dampens the ending, doesn't it?" Bart punned.

"That was terrible!" I laughed in spite of myself.

"I'm sorry. I promise I'll never pun again."

"No, don't!"

"Don't promise or don't pun?"

"Don't promise. I was thinking how tragic the fire was, how depressing for Mom and Dad, and was wallowing in self-pity because my beautiful dress is probably ruined. But it's all just stuff. None of it's important if we're alive."

"Bravo, Allison!" I turned to see Mom and Dad standing in the shadows on the balcony next to Jim and Alma.

"It is all stuff and can be replaced. But you can't," Dad

said in a husky voice. "I came to in the pool with your voice in my head pleading for help. I've never felt so helpless in my life. Then I heard your scream and nearly went mad. We couldn't get out."

Mom picked up the narrative. "Thank heaven I got there when I did with Jim right behind me. We pulled these drowning rats from the pool just in time. Bart was like a madman, fighting to keep your dad from bleeding to death, keep his head above water, and needing to get to you."

Bishop O'Hare joined us on the balcony. "I'm sure the millions who see the news tonight will find the whole thing exciting. Cory Black and company at this moment are rushing the film to the station. Make sure you ask for a copy for posterity. And remember, we have an appointment as soon as you get back from your honeymoon."

Bart laughed. "Wouldn't miss it for the world."

"You still have the front of the house," Jim observed. "Those fire doors and walls we installed between each wing stopped the fire. Other than a few broken windows, I'm happy to report there's no major damage to the living areas. You just don't have any guest rooms, servants' quarters or cabanas left—and I'm afraid your pool and garden aren't in the best shape."

"As you say," Mom shrugged, "it's all stuff. Our most precious thing is still intact—our family. We can celebrate! Tony—and Margo—are dead, the syndicate is dying, my husband can be resurrected, and my daughter finally married her only love."

I turned to Bart. "Thank you, Mr. Allan. I owe my life to you once again." I reached up to kiss Bart's cheek.

"I'll collect my reward later," he grinned, pulling me close. I felt good in his arms.

About the Author

Lynn Gardner describes herself as "someone who can tell a good story." In building the plot and characters of her first novel, *Emeralds and Espionage,* she did extensive research on the countries described in the novel, and carefully gathered information on the FBI and various aspects of the military.

Lynn and her husband, Maurice, make their home in Quartz Hill, Califiornia, where Lynn is a stake family history consultant. They are the parents of four children. Among her many interests, she lists reading, sewing, golf, traveling, beachcombing, writing, family history, and spending time with her four granddaughters.

OTHER BOOKS AND BOOKS ON CASSETTE BY
LYNN GARDNER

Pearls and Peril

Diamonds and Danger

Turquoise and Terrorists